NO HEAVEN FOR GUNGA DIN

NO HEAVEN FOR
GUNGA DIN

consisting of THE BRITISH AND
AMERICAN OFFICERS' BOOK

by ALI MIRDREKVANDI GUNGA DIN
edited, and with an introduction by JOHN HEMMING
with a foreword by PROFESSOR R. C. ZAEHNER

E. P. DUTTON & COMPANY, INC.

NEW YORK   *1965*

But who are ye in rags and rotten shoes,
   You dirty-bearded, blocking up the way?

We are the Pilgrims, master; we shall go
   Always a little further . . .

JAMES ELROY FLECKER

FOREWORD

LIKE GENERAL DE GAULLE, he was unique,—as a man and as a writer. But there the comparison must end. His name was Ali Mirdrekvandi, but he preferred to be called Gunga Din. He was a peasant from the wilds of Lorestan in south-west Iran, and by all the rules he should have been illiterate.

He came to me as a houseboy when I was working in the British Embassy in Tehran : he stayed for about six weeks, then vanished. This is all I saw of one of the most extraordinary human beings I have ever met,—the author of this book.

He seemed to love dirt for its own sake; he was naïve, yet at the same time shrewd; he made you laugh and pretended not to understand why you were laughing, but you wondered all the time whether he was not secretly laughing at you himself.

As a poor peasant he had no right to be literate, and yet he had taught himself to write Persian, how, when, and where I do not know; and then, with the arrival of British and American troops in Iran during the war, he taught himself English too. He taught himself from dictionaries, he taught himself by listening to the soldiers, and he taught himself from the Gospel according to St. Matthew which a considerate Padre had given him. The result is the English of this book,—wildly incongruous yet at the same time touching. He was like that too. I think he knew when he made mistakes, but he just thought that his own way of saying things was better. And who is to say that "infinite

7

beautiful" isn't infinite better than "infinitely beautiful", or that a "steepy" is not infinite more expressive than a "steep slope"?

He came to me shortly after I had become a Catholic, and as is the unpleasing way of converts, I prowled around seeking whom I might devour. Gunga was religious, but he had little love for Islam. What better prey? I took him to Mass: he "had one ton of joy" (he was always very precise with figures). I taught him the Apostles' Creed; he got it right except for two articles. For him "I believe in the communion of saints, the forgiveness of sins," became "I believe in the communion of sins, the forgiveness of saints." In a way he was a saint, and I have no doubt at all that he is forgiven.

He kept in contact with Mr. Hemming until 1949. Since then there has been no word of him. Last year I enlisted the support of the competent authorities in Iran to find out what had happened to him, but so far without result. Now that this book has at last been published I very much hope that all concerned will redouble their efforts, and that Gunga (who never expected anything from anyone) will get his reward at last.

R. C. ZAEHNER

ALL SOULS COLLEGE, OXFORD
14TH MARCH, 1965

INTRODUCTION

Dear Captain,

I have learnt about 1000 words of English during my working. as I had a good interest to learn English, I have agreed with myself I must be destroyed unless to learn it.

I am out of work and cannot learn English without job. I have come here to pray you to give me a job at a British soldier, perhaps during my service to learn English. You may be sure I am very active for work as soon as a work to be given to me and can achieve it very bravely.

You see that I am durty and have no clothing. I have no fault, because a thief has stolen al my clothings. I am waiting the strength of God get into your heart to make you put me on work.

* * * * * * *

By 1943 the explosion of war in Europe had echoed into nearly every corner of the earth. It had echoed across the Middle East, even into the

9

remotest mountains and valleys of Persia. And it was from these distant mountains and valleys, in search of food, in search of work, in search of a means by which they might live better, that some ventured forth, who had hitherto tasted little of twentieth century western civilisation. Word had reached them that the British and American Forces had entered their country, and in the hope that this might mean a more prosperous life some felt it worth making the journey to see. Days that had been spent amid hills and sheep and donkeys and tracks, and nights that had been spent with silent stars and prowling wolves, were now spent in a world of jeeps and M.P.s (Military Police), of compounds, of barbed wire, of hunting for work, a world of potential baksheesh or, if need be, profitable theft. To newcomers from the mountains it was suddenly a world where Man's clocks and not God's sun told you the time, where Man suddenly seemed to have more initiative. And in such a world it was not surprising to see new ambition in the most unexpected heart.

This was Teheran. Here, as in much of Persia, the British and American forces needed civilians to work for them. And here both had their headquarters. Each recruited its own civilians. Each had its office, surrounded by a crouching, leaning, stand-

ing, sitting assortment of humanity, waiting for something to happen. Some quietly de-loused themselves, some slept, some argued. This particular figure had detached itself from the rest and produced a letter, which he claimed to have written himself.

As I read it its author gazed at me with dark round eyes set in a dark round closely shorn head. He certainly was "durty". His clothing was little more than an old sack. His projecting ears were round too. So was his nose. Even his shoulders were round—not that they seemed round through weakness or care—this they were not: his short, stocky body and the naked legs and feet that emerged from beneath the sacking looked extremely strong.

I had already sent him to the local Mobile Workshops as a possible Handyman. But it was not to be. He was back with a second letter.

Dear Sir,

We went to the factory which you presented us for work. I did not see the President of the factory, but the clerk of the factory wich is a Persian man gave me a job that all my friends are Persian man and they don't know English. I thought that I will never learn English here, therefore I did come dear sir. I have promised with myself I *must learn English unless to be killed. You may put me in your prison only my guard be an Englishman. If the spirit of the God comes on you and makes you to give me job at a British man, I can during my service to learn the whole English language within five months. I hope the God make you to give me job.*

Never before had anyone offered a desire to learn English as his reason for applying for work. And now that one had, it was extremely odd that he should be, not a clerical worker, but a man who was apparently as uncouth as the hundreds of totally illiterate coolies who daily thronged every conceivable source of employment.

I sent him somewhere else. But the next day he was back. And when I asked him what lay behind his ambition to learn English, he told me in a voice of extraordinary authority, almost rebuke, that he had to learn it because his heart told him he must.

"It is like a man who smokes much. If he cannot have cigarette, maybe he will do bad things. It is so with me. If I cannot to learn English, it is better I die."

It was then, little realising what would be the outcome, that I promised, whether he found work or not, I would correct any letters he might write to me. After that Gunga—or Ali Mirdrekvandi, as he was until some perceptive American officer re-named him much later—came and went. He could not, it seemed, settle down to any steady job. For a time he worked for the Americans in their camp at Amirabad. Occasionally he brought a new letter for correction. Always he reiterated his ardent desire to learn English. And when at last the winter drove him south to the warmth of the plains, he assured me he would write me letters for correction every few days. Hoping not to lose track of him, I gave him a letter to a colleague in the south and he departed.

Weeks passed. No letters came. I thought I had seen the last of him. But then, quite suddenly, in April he re-appeared. With him came this.

p
a I g *The detailed of travelling*
e *for Excellence Lieutenant*

4/23/44

Dear Best Sir Excellence Lieutenant Hemming,

The first, I give my best petition to omniscient God to grant you the best happiness, a long age and a big VICTORY.

The second, I have been the first to remember

your gently kindness and prettily promise about the English language. I wrote to your Excellence this letter, the detailed of my travelling, to be proven that I could not to write letter to you or to achieve the English language.

Dear master, when you gave me chit, I came down from Tehran to Ahwaz by train in 24 hours. Then I came to Khurramshahr by truck within 6 hours. Straightway I went to the Labour Office in that town and did wait upon your good fellow and offered to him the chit. He was very happy and glad and would titter when he read the note. He surely wanted to help me and give me job, and I believed, for he looked pretty good. But it was my fault. He told me "Come next day." I did so, but when I got into the market, I saw one of my previous fellows. He said unto me, "Ali, fear, fear from God. Shame of yourself, for your brothers and sisters are being hungried. They have no costume, not anything. They have no their daily bread. They are just going to die."

When I heard these words I was very sad, much grieved. Immediately I came at your good fellow and told him I can't work. He repeatedly told me, "Come, I give you work", but I told him I cannot.

Immediately I got forth from Khorramshahr

and came to Andimeshk. And I came to Reihan. Reihan is a village in which my brothers and sisters are living and it is my native place. When I visited my brothers and sisters, I saw that they were wearing nothing. They are so poor that they are eating named ballowt instead of wheat bread. When I saw so I was very angry. I made a big fire and put all my dictionaries into it and then sat down gravely.

When all my dictionaries were burnt and were changed with ashes, I sweared and agreed I shall learn English no more. I had 60,000 rials that day. I immediately bought flour, wheat, cloth and what was necessarity for them. Then I begun to plant the seeds in the ground. I did sow a several days. When my plantership was finished, I saw that my brothers and sisters were very happy and glad, so I was glad too.

Few days went by. I remembered the English language. I was very unhappy why I would burn my dictionaries. My brothers and sisters were asking me about my sadness and I told them about English language. Then they gave me a cow and they told me, "Take this cow to town and sell it and buy one dictionary for yourself and work for five months somewhere you want and give us some *money every pay day, and come and help us when the seed in the ground will be reaped."*

When my brothers said so, I took the cow to DIZFUL. I sold the cow for 500 rials and I bought a dictionary for 200 rials. I started to go to AHWAZ. During my path I was faced with 12 armed outlaws or thieves. They took me away about 60 miles or more away from the road. They wanted to kill me, for they thought maybe I go tell the Government about their guns and their place, but I did swear I shall not repeat to Government. So they left me, but they took my money.

I came from the thief's place not knowing where I am going, for my path was lost. At last I came to a village near AHWAZ. I asked a villager for some bread. He got some for me and asked me, "Can you be a shepherd and watch the animals at this village?" I replied, "Yes, but what is my salary, please?" He said unto me, "There are in this village cows, asses, oxes and donkeys, the total above 120 animals. You will take them to the desert every morning, in those places that there is grassy, and graze them, and watch nobody steal or no wolf kill them, and bring them back every night. Your salary is 2 rials every animal, per month and your food."

I did accept for I had no money. I did take the animals to desert and put them in grassing ground, then I begun to learn English by practice. At last I was guarding the animals for 24 days. I was learning English by dictionary during my working as shepherd. On the day of the 25th there was a fight between the donkeys. I wanted to prevent them from fighting. I did, but when I came back, I saw that the cows have been eating my dictionary. So I was very angry and sad, for the dictionary was useless. There were only 10 or 12 pages leaved. I sadly fell to a sleep.

When I awake I saw that night came and the road to the village is very far away. I immediately took the animals to village. During the road there was an attack by two wolfs. They killed two asses. I gone report to the villagers about the matter. They got angry with me, they finished me and gave me my pay and told me that they don't want a shepherd that he could not kill the wolf. And so I was finishing. And forthwith I came to AHWAZ.

Then, in the morning, I immediately appeared myself for a job at the Labour Office. The Captain and his good sergeant gave me a job as STORE-KEEPER and I worked there for 13 days. What was the reason that I have been finish? I had no dictionary and moreover there was no any person to talk English. I had always to speak Persian or Araby and the old Storekeeper was angry too. At last I was finished. One American Sergeant took me back to his camp. After working and examining me for a few days he took me to the big office and told the Captain, "This man is all right for storekeeper." Then I worked as Storekeeper, my pay 45 rials every day with overtime and my food and the American soldiers would help me and gave me everything as gift. I was very happy for I could learn English by practice. The store was a very big store and the captains and the soldiers were all around me and they would talk English so I could to learn English.

What was the reason I came here and did finish myself? About 7 days ago I got a report about my brothers and sisters telling me, "Our uncle has been killed by another uncle and the murder uncle is selling all our things."

We did not know what is his deciding and I finished. Albeit I knew that my pay will be raised and my job will be raised too according to my sergeant saying.

At last I came to my village and fixed their

differences and made them in peaces. Then I gave money to brothers and sisters. Then I came here to you.

This was my detailed travelling.

My Dear Best, Officious, Philanthropic Excellence Hemming,

I honourably offer myself to your Excellence for a job. Although I could not to achieve the whole English Language at the same abodement time, for my brothers and sisters were caused, I am sincerely able to do and perform these jobs. 1. Mess Servant. 2. Storekeeper. 3. Supervisor. 4. Foreman. 5. Timekeeper. 6. Checker. 7. Groom and Washing Vehicle.

Mess Servant and Storekeeper are my previous job—but I have carefully learnt another jobs by my mind, and looking at anothers, who were working around me.

As I know as officially you are one of the most officious to your native place and to Human, so I believe and am faithful you will give me job.

"Mess Servant" it was to be. Within a few days Gunga was helping to light fires and carry water in our Officers' Mess. He slept among the cockroaches *on some boards and sacks in a disused garage at the side of the building and set up his writing-desk on a disused oven top in the room where he lit the boiler. And it was here among the crude-oil tins and black spiders' webs that he began to write in earnest.*

After a few letters "for correction" I suggested he should write a story instead and he began "Nurafgan"—or "Irradiant" as his hero was called. He wrote and wrote. And in the evenings we would discuss his works and his thoughts. We discussed God, flies, camels, angels, guns, mountains, cherries, the wind, the Shah, the shape of the world, the rich, the poor, the size of the sea. We discussed snakes, Doomsday, prophets, his grandfather and demons, life and death and Jesus Christ. We discussed anything and everything. And still he wrote. Not until the war was over was "Nurafgan" finished. It runs into hundreds of thousands of words and covers thousands of sheets of paper. And it flowed from his pen with scarce a deletion or amendment.

But it is his other book that concerns us here. "The British and American Officers' Book" was begun for the entertainment of the officers, for whom Gunga worked some time later, but whether any of them ever read more than its opening paragraph is doubtful. Before it was finished all the allied forces had left the country. So it is published here for the first time.

It is a fable, and in a sense a prophecy (for it takes place after the Third World War—the Harvesting-Living-War, as he calls it), and it is also a judgment. Its language, like the language of "Nurafgan", is part New Testament, part British Army and part American Army. It is in fact the language of all who knew Gunga in that strange Anglo-American-Iranian world of 1944.

Its content reflects the child in all of us and produces reactions of varying intensity from the adult in all of us. Some who have read it have mumbled of blasphemy and quietly put it aside, saying it was not for them. Some have been convulsed with laughter and utterly charmed. Catholic puritans have loved it, puritan catholics have loathed it. All have found it wholly original.

For my own part I find it a splendid touchstone. Gunga himself was a splendid touchstone. He held as it were the mirror up to Nature, being so natural, so close to Nature himself. And so with this book. It holds up a true mirror—not to the truth of fact, the truth of reason, the truth of the head, but to the truth of the imagination and of the heart, the vision of the child. God's sun was more important to Gunga than Man's clocks, the Milky Way a finer reflector of truth than a motorway, and the workings of Nature herself a far surer guide than any amount of educational instruction or religious indoctrination.

No one can follow this extraordinary journey up to Heaven without an uncomfortable feeling that Gunga's fate at the Judgment Field would more truly be the fate of us all and that the judgment upon his officers would more probably have fallen upon him. But this is not to say that Gunga's vision of God or his fellow-men was false. His whole story rings gloriously true. And it is in this paradox in Paradise that the real value of his story lies. Today we live in a so-called affluent society. It is an apt phrase, for affluence suggests consumption and acquisition rather than creation and dispossession. In such a society, where no one is any longer clothed only in a sack and where we are securely muffled up, not only in ample clothes, but in tradition, form and ceremonious duty as well, it behoves us to think seriously of divesting ourselves of anything which may obscure our vision. Only from the centre of the circle of Life can be seen the universal truth, which looks outward in all directions, surveying our writhing world quietly and naturally and ever unaffected by the distortions of man. Only at the centre lies the unity of the world's multitudinous religious radii. To

*reach it, if we will, undoubtedly demands a painful
journey of self-examination and divestment for us
all. But, on the journey, God's sun may well be a
better celestial signpost than Man's clocks, and
Gunga in a filthy sack a better guide than a robot
in a snow-white gown. So, as you accompany the
British and American officers heavenwards, it is, I
suggest, far more profitable to look upon the adven-
ture, not with the eyes of "General Burke their commander in their front" but with the more child-like
and less worldly eyes of "Gunga Din their servant in
their behind."*

*With this said, 'Open the gate, O watchman of
the night!' and let every pilgrim judge for himself.*

THE BRITISH AND AMERICAN OFFICERS' BOOK

by

ALI MIRDREKVANDI GUNGA DIN

IN THE NAME OF THE FATHER AND THE SON AND OF THE HOLY GHOST AMEN

NOTHING CAN BE DONE WITHOUT GOD'S ASKING OF. NOTHING CAN LIVE WITHOUT GOD'S BLESSING. NOTHING CAN GROW UP WITHOUT GOD'S WILLING.

ABOUT GENERAL BURKE AND HIS MEN ON THE MILKY WAY. . . .

On the evening of the first night of the seventh month, the officers were yet continually going ahead on the Milky Way along under Heaven with General Burke their commander in their front and with Gunga Din their servant in their behind. Suddenly General Burke stopped, saying, "We are yet very far away from Heaven-Gate, I think," and he kept continually on looking to his front with his hands on his loin. All the officers stopped behind General Burke, wiping off their sweats.

"I don't know where the hell we are going. I only know that we have wandered badly on this Milky

Way," said Colonel Asquith and he sat down in the middle of the road.

"Hell, I don't know anything about that, because I am very hungry," said Colonel Wyman and he sat down also.

"I can't walk any more because I am very tired," said Colonel Grant and he sat down.

"I can't walk either, because I am possessed with the same you are possessed with. I mean I am tired," said Major Hemming and he sat down also.

"Well, I am so hungry that I do not know anything about tiredness," said Major Matthews and he sat down saying, "Gunga Din sit down here and clean up my shoes."

So Gunga Din obeyed. Captain Duff looked up to all directions saying, "How infinite beautiful, infinite fine and infinite valuable is the weather of this world! The creatures down on earth will never die if they have such infinite good weather," and he sat down.

"Take it easy please. Talk about hunger; think what has befallen our bellies. I think a piece of dried bread is more valuable than this infinite good weather," said Captain Birch and he sat down also. Major Lawson began to cough saying, "And I don't know what to do. I have not smoked my pipe since last night, because I have finished my tobacco. And,

O, I am so tired that my legs will hold me up no more," and he sat down quickly.

Major Plummer said, "Water is more useful than tobacco; besides being tired, I am thirsty," and he sat down also.

"I am not tired, neither hungry nor thirsty nor anything else, but my head aches, because I have not drunk any whisky since we finished our ration," said Captain Rudd and he sat down.

"I don't know what is the matter with me," said Captain Blore, "I am walking like an old man 200 years of age," and he sat down.

And all the officers said such things and they sat down one after another. But General Burke was yet continually looking to his front.

"We better lie down here and sleep until morning," said Colonel Wyman after a while.

"We will die from hunger if we do," said Major Hemming, "we had better go ahead as much as we can."

"Hell, I can't walk," said Major Lawson. "One of you must pick me up and carry me if you want to go ahead."

But General Burke lifted up his head and said to all the officers, "We must go on, although everybody is tired. Take your rest quickly therefore. We shall start in 30 minutes." And he sat down thinking.

"We shall be wandering a long time, if we exactly have lost the gate of Heaven," said Major Matthews. And Major Lawson said with a loud voice, "I said nine hundred thousand times that we should not leave earth without a map of heaven."

"What are you worried about?" asked General Burke.

"I am worried that we have been possessed with hunger, thirst, tiredness and with many other such damned things, including having no tobacco."

"Don't be worried about that," said General Burke. "It will be fixed up, if God will."

"Perhaps God won't," said Major Lawson.

"Then we can't help it," said the general thoughtfully.

For half an hour the officers thought and talked and looked about them. Then General Burke lifted his left hand up opposite his face, looking at his watch. Then he arose saying, "Okey. Get up." At once all the officers rose up and set out again along the Milky Way with General Burke in command in their front and Gunga Din their servant in their behind. The moon was not in the sky, but the brilliance of the Milky Way, the bluish of the sky and the rays of the stars made everywhere perfectly clear. So they could see about 3 miles in every direction. After an hour's journey they suddenly saw a point

NO HEAVEN FOR GUNGA DIN

down at the right hand side of the Milky Way. And they stopped and looked and saw that the point was surrounded with white cloud, but in the midst of it and on the west side of it was a darkness. General Burke did not know what the darkness was. Colonel Asquith thought it might be a garden.

"How could a garden come down there?" said Colonel Grant. "No. That is not a garden. That, I think, is a deep-darkness, which cannot be seen by the stars' lights."

"I think that darkness is the shadow of a piece of cloud."

"I think that darkness is some small trees or bushes."

"I think Colonel Asquith was right when he said it was a garden."

And the officers said many other such things as they looked down into the darkness. "We must find out," said General Burke at last, and they turned away from the Milky road. Soon they came to the top of a steepy, which was about 2 miles above the darkness on the west side of the point.

"It is a garden," said Colonel Asquith gazing down, "and it is surrounded by a tall wall."

"Then we must go down to it by this steepy," said General Burke.

"We will all fall off and be destroyed if we do," complained Colonel Wyman.

"I don't think so," said Colonel Asquith. "This steepy looks as if it is covered with soft sands."

"There are soft sands up here, but maybe there aren't on its downsides."

"Well there is no other road, so we are obliged to go down by this steepy anyway."

"That's true," said General Burke and he set off down the steepy with the officers behind him. The garden was about 2 miles distant and the way was very hard, so they went down very carefully. They had covered about three quarters of the steepy, when Major Lawson slipped suddenly and went rolling down like a hunted leopard. "Catch me!" he yelled, but by the time the officers had seen what was happening he had rolled into the soft sands some way beneath them. When they reached him they found him unconscious with his face in the sand. With much labour they carried him out from the sand and brought him round.

"O," said Major Lawson, "I think my feet are broken. O!"

"No. Nothing has happened to you. Your feet are all right. Your right foot is hurt slightly. That's all. We have tied it up, so lie down here until we get news from the garden," said General Burke and he added, "Gunga Din, you stay here with the major."

Then all the officers began to walk round the

garden until they came to a gate. Suddenly they were filled with amazement for they saw at the gate a wonderful creature unlike any creature they had ever seen before. And they approached and saluted it. But for five minutes it did not move for it too was filled with wonder, having never before seen a human.

"Can you speak in angel language?" it said at length.

Now the officers had learnt a little of the angel language during their wandering on the Milky Way, so they said that they knew a few thousand words.

"Why are you breathing so quickly? Why are your faces covered with sweats?" asked the wonderful creature.

General Burke answered, "Because we are very tired; we have been walking for a long time."

"Then sit down and take rest," said the wonderful creature.

"Thanks a lot," said the officers and they all sat down at the gate round about the wonderful creature taking their rest. And the wonderful creature's wonder was increasing from minute to minute during his looking at the officers.

"To which world do you belong?" he asked after a while.

And the officers answered, "We don't understand; please speak more clearly."

33

So the wonderful creature asked again, "Whose world are you belonging to?"

"We belong to earth," said the officers.

"O I see. Earth."

"Yes."

"What kind of earthly creatures are you?"

"Beg Pardon," said the officers.

"I mean what kind of earthly creatures are you?"

The officers did not understand the meaning of the word "kind", so they answered and said to the wonderful creature, "We told you that we are earthly creatures."

"I understand that, but I said what *kind* of earthly creatures? I mean are you goats, sheep, cats, lions, birds, snakes, ants, leopards, lambs, bees, camels, horse—"

"Man, Man, we are of the children of man," said the officers repeatedly.

And the wonderful creature asked, "What kind of the children of man are you? I mean are you girls, old men, old women—"

"We are boys of the children of man," answered the officers repeatedly. The wonderful creature looked at the officers one after another until he took Major Curtis in sight.

"I think you are one of the girls of the children of man, are you not?"

34

"Hell, no I'm not," said Major Curtis. "I'm one of the boys of the children of man."

"Then excuse me," said the wonderful creature. He looked at the rest of the officers and then he asked, "Where have you been and where are you going in the middle of the night?"

"We are on our way up to heaven," they explained, "but however far we go we cannot find the gate. We don't know whether we have passed it or how far we have wandered along the Milky Way. And now we have finished our rations and we are grievously hungry and thirsty."

"What kind of things do you usually eat? I mean do you usually eat flowers, leaves, grasses, fruit—?"

"Fruit, please," answered all the officers repeatedly.

"How many boys are you?"

"Eighty-three."

"I can see only eighty-one."

"The other two are up there at the bottom of the steepy; one of them has hurt his foot."

"Well get them here while I get some fruit," said the wonderful creature and he disappeared into the garden. Major Lawson was brought down to the gate and the wonderful creature soon returned with fruit and water in plenty. When they were all filled, he put a kind of grass on Major Lawson's foot and it was at once made whole. Then General Burke lifted up his head. "How far is the gate of Heaven and when will we reach it?" he asked.

"I don't know exactly where or how far it is," said the wonderful creature. "I only know that you will never reach it by walking along the Milky Road, for this Milky Road does not go up to heaven. The Milky Road is only extended along the stars. It goes from one star to another. Moreover this Milky Road is extended throughout the airy-deserts round about the sky, so you had much better not walk along this Milky Road any more."

"Well what must we do?" asked General Burke.

"Well I myself can't help you, but I think you had much better go down to the Holy Office of the Holy Commanders and ask them to help you. I am sure they will, if you go down to them, for they are holy, generous and good. Besides they cannot only speak your own language; they can speak in the languages of all creatures." And the wonderful creature told them many other such things about the Holy Commanders in detail.

"Will you please show us the road down to their office?" asked General Burke.

"Yes I will," replied the wonderful creature. "But you just sleep around here until the morning. Come back then and I will show you."

"Thank you very much," said General Burke. "Do you think we could sleep in the garden?"

"This garden is floorless and arealess and it is called a Cloud Service Station. The clouds descend and pass down from this garden from minute to minute. You would fall off and be destroyed if you got inside."

"By the way," interrupted Major Lawson, "thanks a lot for healing my foot so soon and so quickly. I think you are the skilledest doctor I've ever seen. You can be very sure that you would get thousands and thousands of dollars daily if you went down to the U.S. I mean down on earth. Do you happen to have any tobacco around here?"

"Tobacco?" said the wonderful creature. "I don't understand."

Major Lawson took his pipe in his hand and said, "Tobacco is something like dried leaves. It is a kind of dried leaves. We usually put it into this damned thing, which is called a 'pipe', and smoke it."

"No," said the wonderful creature. "I haven't got anything like that. What happens when you smoke it?"

"Nothing happens; it just makes our tiredness a little less."

General Burke lifted up his head and asked, "Please tell us. Who are these Holy Commanders?"

"There are five Holy Commanders," answered the wonderful creature. "The Wind-Commander, the Cloud-Commander, the Snow-Commander, the Rain-Commander and the Fate-Commander." And the wonderful creature told General Burke many things about the Holy Commanders in detail. And when he had finished all the officers arose and returning to the soft sand where Major Lawson had fallen they lay down and slept.

When the world became morning, they rose up shaking and cleaning their clothes.

"Hell, my nose is full of sand," said Captain Blore.

"So are my ears," said Colonel Wyman.

"Hell, and so is my mouth," said Major Lawson.

"Well," said Colonel Asquith, "we can't object; the sand was softer than a mattress and we all slept well."

When they reached the gate of the garden they found that the wonderful creature had already prepared plenty of fruit. "Eat what you want," he said, "and put the rest in your pockets." They did so and Gunga Din, besides filling his own pockets, filled a bag which he was carrying with him.

"Now come with me," said the wonderful creature and they all followed him. He led them to the South of the garden for about a mile and then turned to the left down a narrow road. After a while he stopped, thinking. Then he turned to General Burke. "I think you are more clever and more skilled than these boys," he said, "I think your knowledge of angel language is better too, so would you look a little further down this narrow road and tell me where it goes."

General Burke soon returned. "As far as I can see," he said, "I think it goes to the east of that point there."

"That's right," said the wonderful creature. "This narrow road goes directly to the east of that point. Now listen to me diligently. When you reach that point the road will take you down to the other side of it. Then it will take you on to a steepy. You go down that, past the Stony-Clouds and straight on until you come to the Holy Point near the Holy Office of the Holy Commanders. So you don't leave this narrow road until you reach the Holy Point. It will take you thirty days to get there if you go quickly. There are plenty of fruit trees on the way so you will be neither hungry nor thirsty."

And the wonderful creature told General Burke many other such things. Then leaving them, he returned back to the garden. And the officers set off towards the east with General Burke their Commander in their front and Gunga Din their servant in their behind. They reached the east part of the point after the world had become night. And they sat down all together in one place eating the fruits which they had in their pockets. But they were not filled. And they called to Gunga Din and they asked him for more fruits. And Gunga Din came near the officers and he gave them fruit. But many of them wanted more so Gunga Din turned his head to General Burke asking him, "Do you want some, General?" And the General answered and said, "No thanks, I am filled. You much better give all the fruits to Major Lawson, for you will have to pick him up and carry him if he remains hungry."

"All right," said Gunga Din and he immediately gave the fruit to Major Lawson. And at last the officers were satisfied and they lay down and they slept. But Gunga Din did not sleep until he had shined the shoes of all the officers. Then he too fell asleep.

When the world became morning they set off again with General Burke their Commander in their front and Gunga Din their servant in their behind. By noontime they had reached the other side of the point and there they found plenty of fruit trees from which they could fill themselves and their pockets. But they wasted no time and hurried on and by suppertime they had reached the top of the steepy. They ate the fruit from their pockets and fell asleep as soon as Gunga Din had shined their shoes. The next morning they began to go down the steepy with General Burke their Commander in their front and Gunga Din their servant in their behind.

"I think this steepy is about one hundred miles long," said Major Mandell.

"More like a hundred and twenty," said Captain Birch.

"Two hundred," said Colonel Grant.

"I don't think it is more than eight-five or ninety," said Major Hemming.

"O Major Hemming, you are dreaming!" said Captain Birch. "It is quite two hundred miles."

"Anyway," said Major Lawson, "it is easier than the Cloud Service Station steepy."

Suddenly Captain Birch gave Major Lawson a push and he rolled about 20 yards down the steepy.

"Now, now!" said General Burke. "No play during walking!"

By suppertime they had covered only about a quarter of the steepy but they still had plenty of fruit so they rested for the night and during the following days passed down the rest of the steepy without incident. When they reached the bottom they found themselves at the edge of the stony-clouds as the wonderful creature had predicted, so they stopped for the night and then continued their journey along the narrow road. For twenty-seven days of walking and twenty-seven nights of sleeping they continued and on the twenty-eighth night they opened their eyes to behold the Holy Point for the first time. And they all agreed that it was the finest, shiniest and most wonderful in goodness point. Millions and millions of pieces of brown cloud were up in the air to the north part of the Holy Point. Millions and millions of pieces of grey cloud were up in the air over the south part of the Holy Point. Millions and millions of pieces of black cloud were up in the air over the east part of the Holy Point. And millions and millions of pieces of green cloud were over the west side of the Holy Point. Millions and millions of pieces of various kinds of clouds were up in the air everywhere round about the Holy Point. Millions and millions of colourless things were up in the air over the Holy Point and millions and millions of sorts of beautiful trees were round about it. And as the officers climbed the Holy Point they marvelled and when suppertime came they found themselves in a small and beautiful pasture. So they stopped and when Gunga Din had shined their shoes they all fell asleep.

It was dark when they awoke for it was yet early, but they began to walk slowly through the beautiful trees and among the beautiful flowers. And the light increased. And suddenly they saw the Holy Office up in the air above them at the top of a flight of a hun-

dred stairs. There was a white pasture in the area
round about the Holy Office. And the white pasture
was covered with white grasses and white flowers.
And the broadness of the white pasture was about
400 feet in all directions. There was a green road
from the east, which crossed the white pasture and
joined the stairs to the Holy Office. And the officers
walked through the white pasture and when they
came to the first stair they stopped, looking up to
the Holy Office. Suddenly the Fate Commander
appeared, walking along the green road. All the
officers withdrew about four feet. They stopped on
the right side of the green road with General Burke
their Commander in their front and Gunga Din their
servant in their behind. The Fate Commander came.
All the officers saluted. The Fate Commander
stopped before them. He began to speak in human
language, in English language, asking, "What are
you children of men doing up here?"

General Burke answered and said to the Fate
Commander, "We have been wandering throughout
the Milky Way for a long time as we wanted to go
up to Heaven, but we have not been able to reach
the gate. Now we have come here to ask you and
your fellows to give us some help."

"I am very sorry," said the Fate Commander, "but
I can't. You had better wait down here and ask the

43

NO HEAVEN FOR GUNGA DIN

other Commanders about it." And he went up the stairs and entered the Holy Office.

The officers waited. Five minutes passed. Suddenly the Rain Commander appeared, walking along the green road. The officers all saluted and the Rain Commander stopped.

"Who brought you children of men up here?" he asked. General Burke explained.

"Sorry, I can't help you. Better ask the other Commanders," said the Rain Commander and went up the stairs into the Holy Office. Five minutes later the Snow Commander came along, but his reply was the same. The Cloud Commander followed, but was too busy to help; he was very sorry but he could not keep the Rain Commander waiting. And he hurried on up the stairs into the Holy Office.

"Hell, none of the damned Holy Commanders are going to help us," said Major Lawson.

"Shut up!" said General Burke. Five minutes passed. Suddenly the Wind Commander came walking solemnly along the green road. The officers saluted and the Wind Commander stopped.

"O Hello, Children of Man," he said. "I am glad to see you. How are you all? Are you happy this Holy morning?"

"We are happy," answered General Burke, "but not much."

"But why not?" asked the Wind Commander.

"We have wandered helplessly through many worlds," said General Burke, "and for a long time we have beaten the Milky Way with our feet, for we thought it would lead us up to Heaven, but we have travelled in vain and now have come to ask for your help."

"Always ready to help," said the Wind Commander. "Did you see the other Holy Commanders?"

"We did," said the General, "but they were sorry they could not help."

"Ah well," said the Wind Commander, "you and your fellows go to the Holy House. Straight down the Green Road. Rest there. Sleep if you want to. Take a bath. Eat anything you want. You will find it all there. I and my fellows will be back some time this evening."

"Thank you very much," said General Burke to the Wind Commander as he began to go up the stairs.

"Thank you too, Children of Man," said the Wind Commander, "I always want to try my best for you." And he went up and entered the Holy Office.

Half an hour's walk brought the officers to the Holy House but when they entered it they were astonished to find nothing inside. They saw no bathroom, bedroom, resting room nor mess-hall, so just stood on the floor of the Holy House thinking.

"Well, there's nothing to eat here," said General Burke. At once the house was turned into a mess-hall, with food for 83 people ready upon the tables. The officers were exceedingly happy. They sat down on the mess chairs at the mess-tables and ate until they were perfectly filled.

"Now," said some of the officers, "we want a bath." At once the mess-hall was turned back to the Holy House and the Holy House became a spacious bathroom. Hundreds and hundreds of various kinds of perfumy soaps and bath clothes were made ready with razors, razor-blades and other such things. The officers took their clothes off and began to shave, every officer his own face. But Gunga Din shaved Major Lawson's face. When they had shaved and bathed, Gunga Din began to shine their shoes. But as soon as he did so, their shoes became new shoes already polished. When he wanted to brush their clothes they became new clothes, ironed in the best beautiful manner.

"Now," said General Burke when all this was over, "we want to sleep."

A large bedroom with 83 beds appeared in the same mysterious manner and the officers were soon fast asleep.

When the world became evening they awoke and rose up and the bedroom was turned again into the

Holy House. Suddenly the Holy Commanders came in, happily shaking the officers' hands and saying, "We will help you and send you up to Heaven." But before the officers could speak their thanks, the Holy House was again turned into a bathroom and the Holy Commanders began to take their bath. The officers washed their faces. This done the bathroom became a resting room and the officers and the Holy Commanders sat down upon the chairs talking and laughing and drinking Holy water. The Holy Commanders sat on the chairs on one side of the resting room and the officers sat on the chairs on the other. Gunga Din was sitting on the last chair, which was behind the door. General Burke turned his head to the Holy Commanders.

"You work pretty hard in your Holy Office," he said. "During our living on earth we heard that the creatures of these worlds never work."

"Ah," answered the Cloud Commander, "we do not work for ourselves. We are only serving the earthly creatures. If the earth were empty of its creatures we would be only too grateful."

"We are sincerely labouring for the earthly creatures all the time," explained the Snow Commander. "We send them snow, rain, wind and weather but regretfully the earthly creatures never say thank you."

47

"Not only they don't say thank you," added the Rain Commander, "but they aren't even pleased with our service. They often behave like madmen and run angrily into their huts or houses when the clouds begin to rain."

"We are obliged to serve them whether they thank or abuse us," said the Wind Commander.

"I'm not," said the Fate Commander. "I work for the earthly creatures just as much as they thank me. Just as they seek for me and love me, so I serve them."

"The earthly creatures are never angry with you," said General Burke, "and I don't think they ever will be. They usually run into their houses lest their clothes get very wet. For if their clothes get wet they get sick and only with many labours can they make themselves dry."

"Well, anyway," said the Holy Commanders, "we shall help you all we can and send you up to Heaven tomorrow morning. Now we want you to explain to us about earthly creatures and their situation on earth. We know most of it but we want to know specially about the children of Man."

"Alright," said General Burke and he explained and his explanations lasted 3 hours and 25 minutes.

"Can you give us another parable about Democracy?" asked the Cloud Commander when he had finished.

48

"Yes," said General Burke. "Democracy is like an infinitely beautiful girl, with whom many people have fallen violently in love, and some crazy people among them. And Oh yes. Here is another one; Democracy is like an infinitely precious coat of mail that does not fit everybody and specially it never fits the wild-people."

And General Burke spoke many like parables to the Holy Commanders.

"Can you give us any more parables about Communism?" asked the Cloud Commander. And General Burke answered, "Yes, I can. Communism is like a wild scorpion, which seriously beats both its friends and its enemies." And he added to the Holy Commanders, "It was you who tried to prevent us from erecting our freedom tent upon earth."

"We?" said the Holy Commanders. "What do you mean?"

"Yes," continued the general. "During the Harvesting-Living-War you helped the enemy by covering everywhere with snow, for the enemy were accustomed to it and we were not."

"We never help earthly creatures of either side during their fighting," said the Holy Commanders. "You won the Harvesting-Living-War anyway didn't you?"

"Yes. In the end," said General Burke.

49

"Then what are you worrying about?"

"I am worried, because before we won thousands and thousands of our beautiful boys were sacrificed. And the reason was that you caused the enemy to give us his most dangerous blow at the beginning of the Harvesting-Living-War. I admit we won in the end and the enemy was destroyed for ever but—"

"Your talks are laughable," said the Snow Commander. "I usually send 10 to 20 Heavenly tons of snow down to earth in one earthly year. During the year of the Harvesting-Living-War I only sent 6 Heavenly tons—less than usual. Perhaps it was the cold wind that helped your enemy. We don't take sides anyway."

"No, we don't," said the Wind Commander. "And I haven't got any cold winds either. You can go and look at my Wind-stations and Weather-service-stations if you like. It's the snow and the seasons that usually make the wind cold."

"I suppose you object to the Fate Commander," said the Cloud Commander. "He usually helps earthly creatures during their fighting."

"I don't do any such thing," said the Fate Commander. "I only do my own business. I didn't help you or your enemies. But you should have kept awake and worked with a forceful faith during Half-peace-half-fear-time so that you might win at the beginning of the Harvesting-Living-Wartime. You should have understood what you should do when you heard your enemies' talks and saw his outwardly doings during Half-peace-half-fear-time."

The Cloud Commander turned his head to General Burke. "When did you leave earth?" he asked.

"We left earth during the earthly year 2084."

"Well, where have you been since then? Did you go to the Judgement Field? Have you got your Freedom Passes from the Judge?"

"No," said the general. "We have been trying to get there for over four years. We have travelled miles along the Milky Road and we stayed with some angels for a few months but they could not tell us the way to the Judgement Field. We knew we had to get Freedom Passes but we haven't got them because we couldn't."

"Then I'm afraid we can't help you," said the Holy Commanders. "We shall be violently wrath-ed if we send you up there without Freedom Passes."

For ten minutes they sat in thought. And the officers' joy was turned into sorrow. Then the Wind Commander spoke.

"You see, the children of Man, who are now up in heaven, all have Freedom Passes with them. When they left earth they went straight to the Judgement Field and got them. We would sincerely help you if

51

we could, but without Passes . . ." He shook his head.

"Well, can you show us the road up to Heaven's gate?" said General Burke.

"If you like," said the Wind Commander, "but you'll never get there walking. The gate of Heaven is seven Heavenly miles up from here and one Heavenly mile is about a hundred million earthly miles, so it's about seven hundred million earthly miles. We wanted to send you up on a piece of cloud —it only takes twelve hours—but without Passes...."

"Can you send us to the Judgement Field on a piece of cloud?" suggested General Burke.

"Too far," said the Wind Commander. "It's twenty Heavenly miles from here. Clouds can't go that distance."

"Could it put us down somewhere near the Judgement Field?"

"Clouds are not allowed to go near the Judgement Field at all," said the Wind Commander, and then turning his head to the other Commanders he said, "I think we had much better send these boys on a piece of cloud somewhere near the gate of Heaven."

"All right," agreed the others. "We'll do that."

"I think that's the best we can do," said the Wind Commander, turning back to General Burke. "We'll send you off in the morning."

When the officers had thanked the Holy Commanders, the Cloud Commander spoke.

"You realise, of course," he said, "that even if you reach the gate of Heaven, the Heaven M.P.'s* will not let you in."

"O we'll think about that when we get there," said some of the officers.

They talked and laughed and drank Holy water until suppertime, when the resting room became a mess hall. And after supper they continued to talk and laugh and drink Holy water until it was nearly time for bed.

The Cloud Commander then addressed General Burke. "I am going to ask you and your fellows three questions," he said, "and I want you to answer them diligently."

"We will answer truthfully," said the general.

"The first question is this. Which of us Commanders is the most beautiful of all? Secondly, whose duty is the heaviest, and thirdly, which of us is most useful to the earthly creatures?"

The Cloud Commander's questions were followed by a silence that remained unbroken for ten minutes as the officers all sat lost in thought. At last Colonel Asquith spoke.

* Military Police.

"Perhaps when we say who is the most beautiful, the others will get angry," he ventured.

"No," said the Holy Commanders, "we shall not get angry. Just answer truthfully."

"We shall have to see your duties," said Major Hemming after another pause.

"You have seen our duties all the time that you have been on earth," said the Cloud Commander. "You have seen rain, snow, rain, wind and weather during your living on earth; those are our duties. I send the clouds down to every corner of the earth. The Snow Commander loads the clouds with snow, the Rain Commander loads them with rain. The Wind Commander blows them to every corner of every world. The Fate Commander has to make some creatures happy and some unhappy."

"Will you let us hold a council outside the room?" asked General Burke.

"By all means," said the Holy Commanders. So the officers arose and left the resting room. And their council lasted 2 hours. When they returned they all sat down and General Burke spoke.

"I'm afraid we shall have to see your duties with our own eyes," he said. "I mean we want to see you actually working in the Holy Office."

"What about the other 2 questions?" asked the Holy Commanders.

54

"We have decided to answer them all at the same time," said the general. The Holy Commanders considered this request for a few moments. Then, "All right," said the Cloud Commander. "You come with us to the Holy Office in the morning and we will send you up to the gate of Heaven when you have answered our questions."

"You will see all the places on earth again, when you come into the Holy Office," said the Wind Commander as soon as all the officers had finished expressing their thanks. "The Holy Office is so Holy that it brings all the down-side-worlds into your sight." And he told them many other such things about the Holy Office and they were very happy. Then the Cloud Commander began to laugh as he remembered world-events.

"You saved many nations during the second war," he explained, turning to Major Hemming. "Some of them were infinitely grateful and obliged for your supreme service to them, but a few of them not only didn't say thank you; they nearly caused you trouble."

"That is perfectly true," answered Major Hemming. "But we did not wait to be thanked by the nations we defended during the war. We only waited to see that the nations could fall on the best living-way."

Captain Duff beat the table with his wrist. "Those

55

few nations who nearly caused us trouble lay down in their countries like a widow during the war, waiting to be eaten up by the enemy. But when we beat the enemy and saved their countries, their tongues were extended against us."

And the Cloud Commander said to the British Officers, "I do confess your nation is the most excellent in anything. One special thing that your nation has most perfectly understood but the other nations have not yet is this. Your nation has understood where it has come from, what it must do during its living on the earth and where at last it should go."

And the Holy Commanders and the officers talked and laughed and drank Holy water for three hours until it was time to sleep. Then the resting room was turned into a bedroom with eighty-eight beds and, after taking off their clothes, they all slept.

Early the next morning when it was yet dark a Holy Voice woke the Holy Commanders, saying loudly, "Get to work." Immediately the Holy Commanders woke the officers and when they had all hurriedly put on their clothes they went out from the Holy House going quickly down the Green Road to the Holy Office. After 22 minutes they had reached the bottom stair of the Holy Office. And a few seconds later they were inside. The Holy Commanders sat down in their special places behind their

Holy desks and they waited doing nothing. The officers sat down on small chairs, which had suddenly appeared round the walls of the Holy Office. And looking down they could see all the corners of the earth.

"Well," said Colonel Asquith to the Wind Commander, when some time had passed, "what are you waiting for? Why don't you start work?"

"We start work when we are appointed to do so," replied the Wind Commander. "Don't be in such a hurry. You will see us at work just now."

"That's good," said Colonel Asquith. "We are hurriedly desireful to see you working. What is the distance between here and earth?"

"Twelve Heavenly miles," said the Wind Commander. "That's about twelve hundred million earthly miles."

"Then how is it that we can see all the places on earth?" he asked.

"O! You *are* of little faith!" exclaimed the Wind Commander. "The Holy Office is possessed with God's blessing, so of course you can see every corner of the earth."

Suddenly they were interrupted by the Holy Voice.

"Make all empty clouds line up throughout the sky," it said to the Cloud Commander and at once

57

he obeyed. The whole sky was covered with empty clouds.

"Load half of the empty clouds with snow," said the Holy Voice, this time to the Snow Commander. "And let a drift of wind blow them to the Snow-Supply-Station," it added to the Wind Commander. "The rest of the empty clouds are to be filled with rain, so drive them to the Rain-Supply-Station."

The Holy Commanders obeyed their instructions at once. The clouds were divided and sent off and filled up.

"Make all the clouds that are loaded with sea-rain get into line across the sky," continued the Holy Voice, "and give a public rain to all place in Europe continually for three hours."

"I want some wind to guide these clouds down over Europe," said the Cloud Commander to the Wind Commander. And at once it was done.

"Make some winds shake the Mediterranean Sea," ordered the Holy Voice. And the Wind Commander did so until the Mediterranean was shaking hardly and waving heavily.

"Turn your face away from that single ship in the middle of the Mediterranean," said the Holy Voice to the Fate Commander.

"Blow a heavy wave over that single ship in the middle of the Mediterranean," said the Fate Commander to the Wind Commander.

58

"That ship is an English ship. Don't let it be wrecked. Please save it," shouted all the officers to the Fate Commander. But the Fate Commander did not answer neither did he listen. He was only doing his business. And the ship was wrecked into the sea and the shipmen left their ship. And swimming in the water were two workers and one pilot. And the officers were filled with sadness as they looked down upon them.

"Turn your face away from the two shipmen but not away from the third, who is the pilot," said the Holy Voice.

"Blow a wave over those two shipmen," said the Fate Commander and the Wind Commander did so. And the two shipmen were choked by the sea.

"Blow the pilot to the west," said the Fate Commander, "he has to be saved."

So the Wind Commander blew the pilot westwards and blew a large board from the east. And the pilot mounted the board and was saved.

Suddenly the Holy Voice came into the Holy Office saying to the Wind Commander, "Make the winds leave the Mediterranean Sea." Immediately the Wind Commander did so. And the sea was quiet.

"Let the heavy clouds give heavy rain over central Persia," said the Holy Voice to the Cloud Commander.

59

"Heavy clouds over central Persia, please," said the Cloud Commander to the Wind Commander. And he obeyed. And the clouds thundered with hail and heavy rain.

"Turn your face away from all those cows in those stables, but not away from the people," continued the Holy Voice to the Fate Commander and added, "now let a heavy wind take the heavy-hail-loaded-clouds over the stables." The Wind Commander complied and the hail fell with such violence that the roofs fell down from the stables and the cows were all drowned. And the Holy Voice continued to instruct the five Commanders. In one village all the gardens were destroyed and 16 women, 20 children, 3 men and all the animals were killed. Then gradually the storms ceased over Persia and Europe and the Holy Voice turned its attention to Canada. Heavy-rain-loaded clouds were guided down by a quick and heavy wind and the air over Canada was turned into thunder and heavenly-electrics for thirty minutes. But the Fate Commander was not instructed to turn away his face from the cattle nor from the people. And when the rains ceased and the pure-white clouds were scattered in the air, the officers wondered greatly, for they saw beautiful and blessful grasses growing up hurriedly in all Canada-places, all Canada-cows walking very hardly and heavily and solemnly into the beautiful and blessful grasses, all with plenty of blessful milk in their breasts, and the thanksgiving of the Canada people was increasing from time to time.

"Now look down at that Arab-man walking along that road beside that river," said the Holy Voice. "He is a poor Arab-man of great faith. He is out of work, he has no money and he is going to New Jersey to find a job."

At once the Fate Commander turned his face in the direction of the man and remained looking at him intently. The officers all watched from their chairs.

Suddenly some angels appeared on the road in front of the Arab-man. They put one hundred thousand dollars in the middle of the road and then disappeared. The poor Arab-man was hurrying ahead with his long thick stick resting on his shoulder. Just as he was about to reach the dollars he said to himself, "I must see how blind people walk." And he closed both his eyes and walked thus until he had passed the dollars by. Then he opened his eyes saying sadly to himself, "I certainly am sorry for the poor blind people. Being possessed with blindness they are in a most grievous position. Even though I am poor and out of work, I am exceedingly glad that my eyes are all right and that I can see the things that God has created. The poor blind people can only hear what God has created. I would be most grateful if God would have mercy on the blind people." And he said many other such things as he walked along.

Suddenly the angels reappeared, picked up the dollars and again put them down in the path of the poor Arab-man. Then they disappeared.

As he was nearing the dollars for the second time, he said to himself, "Well, I have found out how blind people walk. Now I want to see how a man who is both blind and lame walks." And closing his eyes he began to walk lamely until he was past the dollars by about ten yards.

"My sorrow has become two sorrows," he said to himself, opening his eyes; "I am sorry for the blind but I am more sorry for those who are blind and lame for they are very much more unlucky. I thank God that I am all right, even though I am out of work." And he said many other such things as he continued his walking.

Suddenly the angels appeared for the third time and, after placing the dollars again in front of the Arab-man, they disappeared.

"I must see how drunk-men walk," said the Arab-man as he neared the dollars for the third time. And he began to walk like drunk people walk. He fell down a few times and several times he got off the road and he passed by the dollars without seeing them.

"No," he said to himself, "drunk people are not unlucky, neither are they poor, nor has anything happened to them. They are just a little crazy." And he continued his walking, talking to himself and thinking.

Again the angels appeared and put the dollars in front of the Arab-man. Just as he was about to reach them he said to himself, "I wonder how many steps I can run in one hour." And so saying he began to run with whole speed and sped past the dollars without noticing them. And the angels, picking up the dollars for the last time, vanished.

"Now," said the Holy Voice to the Fate Commander, "look down at that young Persian man who is walking along that street. He is a faithful young man and his original desire is to get a very beautiful girl as his wife."

The Fate Commander looked at the Persian young man intently as he continued to walk along the street. Suddenly the door of a house he was passing opened and a beautiful girl came out. She was about the most beautiful of all girls and she fell in love with the Persian young man as soon as she saw him. And the Persian young man stopped when he saw her and fell hardly in love with her.

"Please, come into the house, won't you?" said the girl. "I would like to," said the young man. So the beautiful girl took the Persian young man into her house. And she fed him and said to him, "I would really like to marry you and become your wife as I have fallen heavily in love with you. See, I have studied English, French, German, Ration, Arabian, Armanian and Persian. I am now working in the English-Iranian Oil Co and my salary is 40,000 per month. Besides all these my father is one of the richest Jewish." And the beautiful girl kissed the young Persian man as she said many other such things to him. But the Persian young man rose up and he said to the beautiful girl, "I had fallen in love with you too, but I am in love with you no more, neither do I wish to marry you, for you are a Jewish girl and I am a Moslem—"

"But I love your Moslem religion more than my own religion as I am in love with you," said the beautiful girl.

"I won't marry a Jewish girl," said the Persian young man and he went out from the house quickly.

"Now," resumed the Holy Voice, "Look down at that American boy standing beside the wall in that street. He is of great faith too. There is a heavenly-seed inside one of the pomagranates in that shop nearby. That American boy will become the richest

and the luckiest child of Man if he eats the pomagranate in which that heavenly-seed is."

The Fate Commander turned towards the American boy and looked at him intently. Then without
taking his eyes from the American boy he said to the
Wind Commander, "Blow those white clouds away
from that city and then make the wind cease altogether." And the Wind Commander did so and the
sun shone down upon the city and the warmness of
the sun's rays was such that the American boy began
to sweat. And wiping off his sweat with his handker-
chief he walked along under the shadow of the wall
until he came to the shop where the pomagranates
were. And seeing them he felt thirsty so he bought
a few. And the pomagranate in which was the
heavenly seed was among them. And the American
boy began to eat them and he ate them all save the
one in which was the heavenly seed. And he was
about to eat that too, but he saw that it was a little
bitter. So he did not eat it but cast it down into the
water-brook and walked on in the shadow of the shops.

"There is a heavenly apple among those in the
shop on the opposite side of the street," said the Holy
Voice to the Fate Commander. "If he eats that too,
he will become the richest and luckiest child of Man."

"Send a cold wind down that street," said the Fate
Commander and the Wind Commander did so. At

once the American boy began to feel cold and he crossed the street from the shadow into the sun and looked into the shops as he walked along the foot-pavement. Soon he reached the apple-shop and feeling hungry bought some apples. And the heavenly apple was among them. And he ate the apples one after another until there was but one left. And it was the Heavenly apple. But when he cut it in half to eat it he found that there was a small worm inside. So he did not eat it but cast it down into the water-brook and went on his way.

"Now turn your face away from that market in that town down there," went on the Holy Voice and the Fate Commander obeyed.

It was just noon and the people were closing their shops, some to go to the mosques to say their daily prayers and some to go to their homes for dinner. There was a little boy playing in the market with a match in his hand. He was lighting wood-matches and throwing them away one after another as they burnt. Soon he saw a drift of old papers in the corner of the market, so he set fire to it as he played. And he kept on walking and playing with the matches.

"Please let a drift of wind hold the fire against that shop," said the Fate Commander and the Wind Commander did so. Soon the fire that the little boy had made was guided into the shops and the drift of wind was so heavy that all the shops in the market were alight in a few minutes. Thousands and thousands of people ran to put the fire off but nobody could enter the market.

"Keep on looking at the little boy," instructed the Holy Voice and the Fate Commander did so.

And the little boy was very much afraid, weeping with a loud voice and running this way and that throughout the market. He did not know how to save himself as the fire was attacking him from all directions. But suddenly the door of a shop fell down after it had been burnt and seeing that there was no fire in the shop the little boy ran inside still weeping. He saw that the shop was a jewellery shop so he filled his pockets with jewels during his weeping. He also took his trousers off and filled them with jewels too.

"I want more wind," said the Fate Commander; "the fire must be increased as the people are going to put it out." And the Wind Commander obeyed. The wind blew so heavily that the fire increased greatly and the people began to flee away. But the fire-machine was working hurriedly. And the fire left one corner of the market so that the little boy might flee. So the little boy picked up the jewels and his trousers and running out of the market, he fled to his home. And the fire was not put off until it had turned the whole of the market into ashes.

And so the Holy Voice came into the Holy Office from time to time and gave such orders to the Holy Commanders. And the Holy Commanders obeyed, until at last at three hours past noon the Holy Voice came into the Holy Office and said to the Holy Commanders, "Now go to your Holy House."

So the Holy Commanders as well as the officers rose up and they came out from the Holy Office. And they came down the stairs, going to the Holy House along the Green Road. And when they entered the Holy House it became a mess-hall and they all ate their dinner. Then the Holy House was turned into the resting room and they all sat down, every one in his own chair, talking and laughing happily. After some minutes had passed the Holy Commanders said to General Burke, "Now that you have seen our duties go ahead and answer us our three questions."

"Yes," replied General Burke. "We have seen and noticed your duties and we will answer your questions in a few minutes. We just want to hold a short council outside the room."

And the officers rose up and they left the resting room and they took council and their council lasted two hours.

"Well," said the Holy Commanders when the officers had come back into the resting room.

"Well," said General Burke, "I confess and all the officers confess with me that the Wind Commander is the most beautiful of all, his duty is the heaviest duty and he is more forceful than all you are . . ."

At once all the officers clashed their hands and applauded happily. And the Wind Commander applauded too and he shook all the officers' hands saying to them, "Now you are all my dear friends and I love you." And he said many other such things to them happily. Then he sat down in his place.

The other Holy Commanders turned to General Burke saying, "You must prove your answers to the three questions, you know."

"All right," said the General, "I will. The Wind Commander *is* the most beautiful of all as we have seen and confessed; his duty is the heaviest and he is more forceful than you are. See, the creatures down there on earth don't need rain every day, neither do they need snow all the time. But they need change of weather and wind all the time. The creatures down on earth can live without rain and snow for a long time, but they can't live without the wind. The Wind Commander is very much more forceful than you are for this reason, that you need him to help you during your working in the Holy Office when he does not need you to help him. You could not send the clouds down to earth unless you asked the Wind

Commander to give you wind. Not only do we confess the Wind Commander's duty to be the heaviest; all the earthly creatures believe firmly that his duty is the highest, the most forceful, the most useful and the most valuable of all."

"It is the coldness of the wind that destroys all the corn and grasses in the winter season," said the Snow Commander. "It is only because I cover them up that they are saved."

"I have told you before that I have no cold wind," said the Wind Commander. "It is the snow that makes the wind cold."

"All right," said the Cloud Commander to General Burke. "If the Wind Commander is the most beautiful of all, his duties are the heaviest and he is more useful and forceful than we, tell us which of us is the least beautiful, has the least duty and is least forceful."

Again the general decided to hold a council outside the room. It lasted one hour. When all the officers had sat down in their chairs, General Burke spoke.

"I firmly believe," he said, "and my officers believe with me that the Fate Commander is less beautiful, less forceful, less useful than the rest of you and that his duties are least. During our council we have taken into consideration all your duties from the time that God created the earth until now."

"Your taking council is wrong and your answers are wrong and laughable," said the Fate Commander. "It is very bad of you to say that my duty is least. How is it that you are not ashamed to say such talks against me, when I caused that you became a general. When Adam began to walk on earth he had not anything with him and looked like a crazy. I caused his children to be skilled in thousands and thousands of various knowledges. I caused the children of man to discover all sorts of mines in various parts of the earth. I caused the children of man to walk in the air like birds and have authority over the sea, the land, and over earthly creatures. I have caused all the children of man's happiness down there on earth."

"I cannot be ashamed," answered General Burke, "because all my answers are perfectly truthful. And anyway you are less beautiful and less useful and your duties are less heavy than the others."

"It is your talks that are laughable," said Major Hemming to the Fate Commander. "Your talks are all about your goodnesses to earthly creatures and you have hidden all your evilnesses. Your evilnesses to earthly creatures are about 96 times more than your goodnesses are."

"And let me tell you something," said Colonel Asquith. "About ninety-nine hundredths of the earthly creatures are your enemies. They would give you trouble if they saw you with their own eyes; they say all the time that you cause all their trouble."

"Now," said Major Lawson, "I know that it is you who are my famous foe. I was sincerely serving in the U.S. Army in both wars and according to my supreme services I should have become a general-marshall at least. But regretfully my rank was not increased at all. I remained in this damned majory-rank and you caused it all!"

"I have known you as my dangerous enemy from the old days," said Gunga Din. "You caused me many troubles during my living down on earth. I was not worried and I held my patience firmly, but one grievous thing that made me and yet makes me very worried and sad is this. I wanted to serve both the British and American Forces with an infinite manner during the Harvesting-Living-War according to the greatest decision which I had taken during the half-peace-half-fear-time. But regretfully when the Harvesting-Living-War started, I could not reach the British Army, neither could I reach the American Army. So I could not serve either and my greatest decision was turned into a drift of sorrow-fire in my heart, which burns me yet. You caused that!"

"Everybody on earth abuses you all the time,"

said Captain Birch. "Everybody is greatly mad and angry with you."

"So you think that the Wind Commander will help you, if I turn my face away from you?" said the Fate Commander.

"Of course he will," said the Wind Commander.

"Sure he will," said all the officers.

"The Wind Commander won't be able to help you if any of us gives you any trouble," the Cloud Commander declared.

"Oh yes, he will," said General Burke.

The Cloud Commander turned to the Wind Commander. "Are you going to help these boys, for we must give them some trouble?"

"You won't be able to give them any trouble," said the Wind Commander, "for I intend to help them in my best manner."

"We shall see about that," said the Cloud Commander. "I shall make the heavy clouds pour heavy rain with storm, heavy snow with heavy storm and heavy hail with storm on these boys right away."

"And I shall turn my face away from them from now on," said the Fate Commander, and so saying he rose up and went out from the resting room.

And the Cloud Commander said to the Wind Commander, "We shall send these boys by a piece of cloud down there on to one of the points right away.

73

Then I know what I shall do with them." And he rose up and went out from the resting room.

The Snow Commander rose up saying, "I am loading the heavy clouds with heavy snow and heavy hail." And he went out from the resting room.

Then the Rain Commander rose up, saying to all the officers, "I am loading the heavy clouds with heavy rain blended with heavy storm." And he went out from the resting room.

"Don't be at all worried," said the Wind Commander as he rose up. "The Holy Commanders won't be able to give you any trouble, if you just listen to what I am telling you. A piece of cloud will take you and put you down on a point about one hundred earthly miles below this Holy Point. When you get down there you must hold on to the trees firmly. You must firmly bosom the roots of the trees and firmly hold the tree roots into your hands and into your feet, so that the heavy winds do not take you up into the air. I will make the heavy wind defend you by taking the snow, rain and hail away from you and away from round about you. So you just try pressing yourselves to the tree roots."

And the Wind Commander gave them many other such orders and then went out from the resting room.

Suddenly the resting room became the Holy House and the officers went outside. Soon a piece of cloud descended and took all the officers into the air after they had mounted it. It took them down to a point about one hundred miles below the Holy Point. And having put them upon it, the cloud left them. The officers kept themselves firmly to the roots of the trees. They took the tree-roots firmly to their bosoms just as the Wind Commander had told them. Every officer had taken a tree-root into his bosom so firmly that it was as if they had bosomed 83 beautiful girls instead of 83 tree-roots. Ten minutes passed. Suddenly millions and millions of pieces of heavy clouds, full of heavy rains and storms, appeared in the air above the officers. And the clouds began to pour down the heavy rains hurriedly upon the officers. But suddenly a heavy wind began to blow very fast, taking the rains and the storms up and away. For one hour the rains fell, but no rain, neither any storm, was poured upon the officers, for the heavy wind took them up and away. Twenty minutes passed. And it became dark. And suddenly the air over the officers was filled with heavy clouds loaded with heavy snow. And the snow was poured down so quick and so offensive as if a Wooly-world had unexpectedly been created round about them. But the wind blew and the clouds could not stay, neither could they take aim at the officers. Suddenly some black clouds came opposite the lights of the stars and opposite the moon light, so that the point, on which the officers were, fell into a very black darkness —so black that the officers could not see each other, neither could they see the nearest things. But a heavy wind came and drove the clouds away, and the point on which the officers were was clear in the light of the stars and the moon. And the clouds continued to drop heavy snow but they could not make the officers wet. Again twenty minutes passed. And then there came millions and millions of pieces of black cloud loaded with heavy hails that came with offensive thunder into the air over the officers. And the hails were as heavy as stones but an infinite quick and offensive wind began to blow. And it blew as if that point had been condemned into destruction; not only did it blow the hails away, it also took the trees up by the roots. It looked as if the point on which the officers were was pouring the hail into the black clouds. Thousands and thousands of trees were broken or uprooted in a few minutes. And the officers began to be afraid. For they could neither see nor hear one another because of the shrieking of the wind and the darkness of the night. Suddenly Major Lawson's tree was taken out by the roots and up into the air with Major Lawson on it. And Major Lawson was hopeless of his life when he found himself in the air taken this way and that with his tree in his bosom.

And one hail struck Major Lawson so offensively in the back that he let go his tree and fainted. He was blown upwards for about a mile but then a drift of wind brought him down to the point where the other officers were and there it held and pressed him continually to the ground. And some of the other officers fared likewise, but a drift of wind saved them and held them firmly to the ground. And the black clouds poured hail for 3 hours and 35 minutes and it was thirty minutes before midnight when the storm ceased. But no hail had fallen on the officers. And there was silence.

Suddenly a piece of cloud descended and took all the officers back to the Holy Point. Major Lawson was brought round but his back ached a little. So when they arrived at the Holy House they all entered and waited.

Suddenly the Holy Commanders came in. "Did you see how I helped you and saved you?" asked the Wind Commander happily.

"Thank you for your valuable braveness," answered all the officers. But before they could continue their conversation the Holy House was turned into a bathroom and the Holy Commanders as well as the officers took a shower after they had taken their clothes off. This done the bathroom became a mess-hall and they all ate their supper.

77

As they were sitting talking, laughing and drinking Holy water, when their supper was over, Major Lawson turned to the Fate Commander and said in a loud voice, "I think you turned your face away from me while those black clouds were pouring down heavy hails. I was taken up into the air when my damned tree was uprooted. I was hopeless of my damned life until a drift of wind saved me."

"I turned my face away from all of you," said the Fate Commander, "but you were all saved in the end."

"You had much better turn your face away from me for ever," said Major Lawson. "You have all always brought earthly creatures bad luck."

"Don't worry about earthly creatures," replied the Fate Commander, "but think how you are going to get up into Heaven."

"I shall not let any piece of cloud take you anywhere near the gate of Heaven," said the Cloud Commander. "And this time the Wind Commander can't help you as he is not the commander of the clouds."

"We shall send you up there on a piece of cloud first thing to-morrow morning," the Wind Commander reassured the officers.

"Well, I'm not going to give these boys a ride," repeated the Cloud Commander.

78

"Oh yes you are," said the Wind Commander.

"Oh no, I'm not, you can't order me."

"You are, because you promised. I am not ordering you."

"Whether I promised or not, I am NOT giving these boys a ride."

"You most certainly are. You—"

"Wait until the morning," said the Cloud Commander, "and you will see for yourself."

"All right," concluded the Wind Commander. "Leave it until the morning."

There was a pause, broken at length by the Cloud Commander. "Some of your fellows are not so joyful as they were last night," he said to General Burke. "They look rather worried."

"They are not worried whether you will give them a ride or not," said General Burke. "They are worried and sad about the British ship, which was upset in the Mediterranean Sea this morning."

The Cloud Commander turned his head to the Fate Commander, saying to him, "As we want these boys to be exceedingly joyful while they are with us, why not explain to them why that British ship was wrecked, so that they may be comforted."

"That British ship left a Communist harbour last night," said the Fate Commander, "and it had some Communist-muds on its undersides, so it was

79

wrecked. The two shipmen died because they had cleaned neither their shoes nor their clothes from the Communist-dusts. The pilot had done so and was therefore saved; he was picked up by an American ship this afternoon."

When the officers heard this, they were exceedingly happy. But General Burke turned to the Fate Commander and said, "Communism was destroyed during the Harvesting-Living-War. What do you mean by a Communist harbour? Has Communism grown up on earth again?"

"No," said the Fate Commander, "there's no Communism on earth now—you are quite right about that—but there are some places which still smell with the smell of Communism." And he explained many other such things.

"Now," said General Burke to the Cloud Commander, when the Fate Commander had finished, "tell me, are you angry with us?"

"No," answered the Cloud Commander, "we are not angry with you. We just want to see how the Wind Commander will give you a ride. We are not like earthly creatures. Earthly creatures sometimes get angry, but we are never angry with anybody."

And so they continued to talk joyfully and drink Holy water until two hours past midnight. And their talks were so much that I am unable to write them in this book in detail.

When the world became morning, the Holy Voice ordered them to get to work and soon afterwards the Holy Commanders set off along the Green Road to the Holy Office with the officers behind them. They had soon ascended the stairs, entered the Holy Office and sat down, the Holy Commanders at their Holy desks and the officers in the chairs prepared for them. After half an hour the Holy Voice came into the Holy Office saying to the Wind Commander, "Let a medium wind blow throughout North America all to-day." The Wind Commander did so.

"It's going to be damned cold in Chicago," said Major Lawson, "too damned cold to work. The people down there'll—"

"Let heavy-clouds pour heavy rain throughout England for forty minutes," interrupted the Holy Voice and the Cloud Commander obeyed, saying to the Wind Commander, "Heavy-clouds over to England please."

"Not unless you promise to give these boys a ride," answered the Wind Commander unexpectedly.

"I can't do that," said the Cloud Commander.

"Then you shall have no heavy-wind to take your clouds down."

"It's not my business to give these boys a ride," said the Cloud Commander, beating the Holy desk with his hand.

"It is your business and no one else's."

"Heavy-rain throughout England for forty minutes," repeated the Holy Voice firmly.

"I said guide these heavy-clouds over England," said the Cloud Commander.

"Not unless you promise to give these boys a ride," answered the Wind Commander, "and drop them somewhere near the gate—"

"I will NOT," insisted the Cloud Commander.

"Then I won't either," said the Wind Commander.

Suddenly the Holy Voice again came into the Holy Office, saying thrice to the Cloud Commander, "Hurry up. Send heavy-clouds loaded with heavy-rain to all parts of England for forty minutes."

"Can't you hear the Holy Voice?" said the Cloud Commander, turning desperately to the Wind Commander.

"I can," replied the other unmoved.

"Then what are you waiting for? Why don't you send a wind to guide those heavy clouds down over England?"

"Because I am waiting for you to send a piece of cloud to take these boys up to the gate of Heaven."

"I said I will NOT. You can't order me nor have you any right to let the Cloud services get behind schedule. You are obliged to guide these clouds down," said the Cloud Commander with a loud voice inclining towards anger.

82

"Not unless you promise to send these boys on a piece of cloud—"

But the Holy Voice interrupted. "Send the heavy rain over England," it ordered the Cloud Commander, "and then do what the Wind Commander says."

"All right," agreed the Cloud Commander to the Wind Commander. "I'll do it."

"Thank you very much," said the Wind Commander. "And now I shall be delighted to despatch your clouds."

As soon as he had spoken the storms over England began and the rains fell heavily on all England-places.

"And now," said the Cloud Commander, "if you would be good enough to wait outside the office for a few minutes, I'll get a piece of cloud to come and pick you up."

"We are not very comfortable that you are giving us a ride," said General Burke, "because you and the Wind Commander are angry with each other."

"Oh no we are not," laughed the Cloud Commander and he and the Wind Commander kissed each other's faces.

Then the Holy Commanders shook all the officers by the hand and bade them farewell and the officers descended the stairs to the Green Road and waited.

83

After two minutes the Wind Commander came out of the Holy Office and standing by the door he said with a loud voice, "A piece of cloud will pick you up right away. It will put you down somewhere near the gate of Heaven and then leave you. But don't forget to tell your situation in detail to the M.P. on the gate. I am sorry you are leaving us but I hope you will all enter Heaven and be happy therein. We would like to see you again, although I know that Heaven-happiness makes you forget about every-'thing."

"And I hope you get your Freedom Passes," added the Cloud Commander, coming out of the office. And the other Holy Commanders came out and shouted farewell messages down the stairs.

"And don't turn your face away from us," said General Burke with a loud voice to the Fate Commander.

"All right," said the Fate Commander, "I will look at you in any times of trouble."

And the Holy Commanders, saying their last good-byes, returned to their office. And the officers waited until a piece of cloud appeared and took them into the air. And it was just noontime when it put them down on a road near the gate of Heaven. And having put them down, it left them and turned back whence it came.

And the officers began to walk quickly towards the gate of Heaven with General Burke their Commander in their front and Gunga Din their servant in their behind. And they reached the gate of Heaven after the world had become suppertime.

"Where are you children of Man going?" asked the Heaven M.P., who was standing at the gate.

"We are too tired and hungry to answer that," said some of the officers sitting down opposite the M.P. and breathing quickly.

"Show me your Freedom Passes, if you want to go in," said the M.P. when he had given them time to recover. And then the officers described to him their situation in detail and their explanations lasted one hour.

"Well, well, you can't come into Heaven as you have not got your Freedom Passes and you have not yet been judged," said the M.P., when the officers had finished.

"Then what must we do now?" asked General Burke.

"I don't care; I think your statements about your position are untruthful. Perhaps you are some of the Hellishes, you have fled out from Hell and now you want to get secretly into Heaven."

"Our statements are perfectly truthful, you can be quite sure of that," insisted General Burke. But the

Heaven M.P. answered saying, "I can't do anything for you. Nobody has ever come here without a Freedom Pass. You are the first party of the children of man that has ever come up here without them."

"Well, will you get us something to eat," asked Major Lawson, "as we are very hungry?"

"There is plenty of food and eatables inside the gate, but you can't go in, neither can you eat them because you have no Freedom Passes. If you had them I would certainly feed you."

Colonel Asquith turned to the M.P. and said, "Heaven has been created for children of man and we are the children of man, so you can't make us wait round here with hungry stomachs, neither can you prevent us from going in."

"Both Heaven and Hell are created for the children of man," replied the M.P. "Those children of man who get Freedom Passes get into Heaven, those who can't are imprisoned in Hell."

"We can't go to the Judgement Field as it is infinite far away and we have nowhere else to go, so we are obliged to wait round here unless you can show us somewhere hereabouts we can dwell in for the present."

"You can't live anywhere round about Heaven," said the M.P., "because all the deserts, forests and other places just outside are covered with immovable clouds. You can't live or wait round this gate because I shan't let you. Your best plan is to go to the Judgement Field even though it is very far away."

"Well, let me see your captain," said General Burke.

"I can't do that," replied the M.P. "Our captain can't help neither can anybody else. Even Messenger-Gabriel can do nothing for you without a Freedom Pass. You better get up and go away. I can't let you keep on sitting here."

"Hell!" said General Burke angrily and he rose up. And all the officers rose up and set off with General Burke their Commander in their front and with Gunga Din their servant in their behind. They walked towards the West, inclining slightly in the direction of the Heaven-walls. But the M.P. shouted after them with a loud voice, "Don't draw yourselves near to the Heaven-walls. Heaven M.P.s are walking round and they'll break your necks if they see you."

But the officers did not listen to what the Heaven M.P. said. They continued to walk westwards under the walls of Heaven until they were about an earthly mile from the gate. Then they sat down together, some with their backs to the wall, thinking.

"The trouble is," said Colonel Grant, "that we can't be sure that we will get Freedom Passes, even if we do manage to reach the Judgement-Field. We would go there however far away it might be, if we knew we were certain of getting our Passes. The trouble is that the Judge will judge us according to our sins; of course one can't help doubting whether—"

"O, you're crazy!" said Colonel Asquith. "How can we reach the Judgement Field? We aren't birds or clouds; we haven't got an airforce to take us there!"

"None of us will get Freedom Passes if we do get there," observed Major Matthews. "We shall all decisively be condemned into Hell, so we had much better forget about going to the Judgement Field even if it is very near."

Colonel Wyman turned his head to Major Matthews, saying, "Oh, you crazy boy! What have we done, what is our sin that we shall be condemned into Hell for ever?"

"I know that we are sinful," persisted Major Matthews.

"No, we have not committed any sin," said Colonel Wyman, but General Burke interrupted, saying, "We shall not go to the Judgement Field even if it be round here, neither shall we agree to go there if the Heavenly M.P.s or anybody else forces us to."

"Well," put in Major Lawson, "the children of man must be gathered together on the Judgement

Field upon the Judgement Day according to what the Holy Bible says. And the Judgement Day has not yet come. It is very far away, I think, and the children of man are not yet gathered together. Some of them are still scattered throughout the damned earth and are still alive and some of them are here in Heaven, so what the hell does the M.P. want us to go to the Judgement Field for?"

And the officers talked of many such things for about one hour. Then they lay down and slept. But the voices of the Heavenly Choir would not let them sleep well and when two hours passed—I mean it was a quarter past eleven o'clock—Colonel Asquith awoke saying, "Hell, I am so hungry that I can't sleep."

"O, I am very hungry either," said Major Hemming, waking up.

"It's thirst that prevents me from sleeping," said Colonel Grant.

"These Heavenly Choirs too," complained Colonel Wyman, and General Burke said, "It is too much thinking that keeps me awake."

Soon all the officers were awake and when the General saw it he determined to take immediate action.

"We must fix these damned M.P.'s up," he said. "We can't wait about starving any longer."

And he rose up and set off towards the gate of Heaven with all the other officers behind him.

"If you don't feed us or let us go in," he said loudly to the M.P. without waiting to be challenged, "we shall go straight in without permission."

"I shall not feed you or let you in," replied the M.P. quietly.

"Then we shall go in by force," said General Burke.

"I shall break your necks, if you don't go away."

But before he could say more General Burke had kicked him down and all the other officers were on top of him. They tied him up and gagged him and then passed through the Gate of Heaven. They turned to their left and soon found a garden filled with various fruits. So they ate and were filled. But they had hardly finished eating when they were set upon by hundreds and hundreds of Heaven M.P.s. A short fight ensued. The Heaven M.P.s did not want to hurt the officers or give them any trouble. They only wanted to catch them. But the officers were beating the M.P.s and showed them no mercy. And the fight lasted 18 minutes. Then all at once the officers fled out of the gate with the M.P.s after them. For half an hour they chased them. And they caught Major Lawson and Colonel Wyman, but the remaining officers after filling their pockets with stones made a counter-attack, pelting the M.P.s until they released their two prisoners. But the M.P.s continued their pursuit for two hours and not until they had lost the officers in a drift of cloud did they return back to the Gate of Heaven.

Now when the officers found themselves no longer pursued, they lay down and slept. And they slept until half-past nine, when they were awakened by the severe voice of General Burke. "Gunga Din," they heard him say, "That Holy House has made you lazy. You are still hoping that the shoes will all be shined by God's blessing!"

"Yes," said some of the officers when they heard this. "Get on the ball and shine our shoes."

Immediately Gunga Din began to shine all the officers' shoes. This done, the officers climbed to the top of the drift of cloud and stood there for some time talking, thinking and looking in all directions.

"It seems to me," observed General Burke at last, "that the places outside Heaven are more beautiful and pleasurable than the places inside. See how beautiful are the places round here and how infinitely good the weather is. We are not certain of getting Freedom Passes if we go to the Judgement Field, so I suggest we forget about going to Heaven or Hell and settle down in one of these beautiful places just outside Heaven."

And they held a council together and the officers agreed with the suggestion of the general. So they came down from the drift of cloud and set off towards the north west of Heaven. By evening they had reached a great white forest quite near to the walls of Heaven. And they ate the fruits as they walked. And their progress was slow, for the white trees of the forest were joined one to another and there were many branches. They walked one behind another lest any of them might be lost. And the white trees were thousands in their variety, but no earthly tree was in that forest save the pomegranate tree. And the pomegranate tree was white also. And the forest contained about three million white trees in all, some of them so high and so thick with leaves that the officers could not see the air above them. And there were many white flowers also.

When night came they tried to sleep but the Heavenly choirs prevented it, and the following morning they continued their journey. At noon they stopped and, choosing a place to dwell in, began to work hurriedly. And every day they worked from morning until evening, some felling trees, some making bricks of mud and some building wooden huts. Some made narrow roads through the white forest and some prepared dry fruits. By the time two months had passed they had prepared many wooden huts and had finished them with every necessity. They had built many paths through the forest and one directly from their huts to the wall of Heaven. And thus they lived continually in the great white forest.

One day when they were walking in the white forest, some of the officers found themselves under an exceptionally tall tree. General Burke suggested that they might be able to see inside Heaven from the top of it, so some of them began to climb up. It took them an hour to reach the top and even when they did reach it they could not see over the walls of Heaven, for the walls were higher than the tree. And when they wanted to come down they found that they could not do so. They tried until nightfall but they were not able to descend one step. And they began to be afraid. They bosomed the branches lest they should fall off in the darkness, but they could not come down. The other officers who were on the ground went sadly to their huts and they gathered together in one hut, thinking diligently how they might save their fellows. They could neither sleep nor eat and they sat in thought until two hours after midnight. Then suddenly all the other officers came in happily.

"A kind and gentle voice came out from above the

Heavenly choirs," they said, "and made us so exceedingly dareful that we all came down from the tree
in less than 20 minutes!"

And so the officers continued to live in the white
forest. I am not able to write in this book all about
the situations and actions of the officers during their
living in the white forest, nor about the manner of
their living. I only know that they were living in the
white forest for eight earthly years and that they
were called the "Outlaw Children of the White
Forest." They could not be caught, neither could
their huts be discovered, so the Heaven M.P.s had
much trouble for eight years. The officers had 8043
attacks on the Southern Borders of Heaven, which
besides being successful caused the Heaven M.P.s
much anxiety.

One morning on the first day of the first month of
the ninth year, the officers were sitting together in
one of the huts, planning their 8044th attack.

"We shall attack at half past ten this evening,"
said General Burke when the plans were complete,
"and we shall not withdraw until three o'clock and
thirty minutes after midnight. So we must get plenty
of sleep now." And turning his head to Major Lawson, he added, "You will walk round and keep watch
over the huts all day."

"O.K. Glad to," said Major Lawson. And all the

other officers rose up and went to their huts and to sleep.

* * * * * * *

News in Adam's House in Heaven

It was about half past ten in the morning. Adam was sitting in his Resting room in his Heavenly house and his wife was sitting beside him. Suddenly a Captain, the Provost-Marshal of the Heaven M.P.s, came in. He saluted Adam and his wife and said, "The Outlaw Children of the White Forest are your children. We can't let them into Heaven as they have not got Freedom Passes. And I can't give them any trouble as they are your children. They have made eight thousand and forty-three small and large attacks on the South Borders of Heaven and they have given my M.P.s a great deal of trouble." And having told Adam many other such things he added, "I and all my M.P.s would be very grateful if you would get Freedom Passes for the Outlaw Children of the White forest, for, after all, they are your children."

Adam thought for some minutes, then he lifted up his head and said to the Provost-Marshal, "All right, I shall fix this up. I shall go and see the Outlaw Children of the White forest."

"Thanks a lot," answered the Provost-Marshal of the Heaven M.P.s and bowing down he went out.

And Adam and his wife rose up and came out from their Resting room. And they mounted a Heaven Plane. And it flew into the air in the direction of the White forest.

* * * * * * *

News in the White Forest

It was morning and it was half past eleven. The officers were still asleep in their wooden huts on their wooden beds. But Major Lawson was walking round the huts and watching. Suddenly the Heaven Plane descended on to the ground in front of the huts and Adam and his wife dismounted.

"Who goes there?" said Major Lawson as they approached.

"I am Adam," said Adam. "Where are my other children?"

"Asleep in their damned beds," said Major Lawson. "I'll wake them up." Then running to the huts he shouted, "Get out of your damned beds. Get on the ball!"

At once all the officers awoke and seized their wooden cudgels, thinking that they had been attacked by the Heaven M.P.s. But Major Lawson

96

shouted, "You can leave your damned cudgels; we are not being attacked. A gentleman's come in a thing like an aircraft and there's a lady with him. He says he's Adam."

So the officers left their cudgels. And coming out they bowed themselves down before Adam and before his wife. And he drew near and kissed them. And his wife did likewise, kissing the faces of their children. Then the children took their Father and Mother into their wooden resting-hut and seated them upon a wooden settee. And sitting round about them, they told their Father and Mother all their situations in detail. When they had finished it was three o'clock in the afternoon and Adam, looking down upon them, said, "Your faces show me that you will get Freedom Passes from the Judge, so I will ask Messenger-Gabriel to send you to the Judgement Field by Heaven Plane. I myself was unable to enter Heaven without a Freedom Pass, so you will not be allowed to either. Besides all my other children who are up here have got them. Your going down to the Judgement Field does not mean that you are sinful; it is just that all my children have to see the Judge before they enter Heaven. You can be quite sure that you will not be condemned to imprisonment in Hell, so you can go to the Judgement Field with great faith."

"Will the Judge judge us for our attacks on Heaven and the Heaven M.P.s during the eight earthly years that we have been living in the White forest?" asked General Burke a little nervously.

"No," answered Adam. "Most certainly not. You will only be judged on your deeds during your lives on Earth."

And Adam spent the rest of the day with his children, eating the dried fruits which they had prepared, looking at their wooden huts, comforting and advising them and exhorting them to refrain from any further attacks on Heaven. Then, when evening came, they returned to their Heaven Plane and after bidding the Outlaw-children farewell, flew off in the direction of Heaven.

No sooner had they gone than the officers began to sing, play, and dance, rejoicing happily in the small field they had made just in front of their huts. But Major Lawson did not play, neither did he dance. He just stood at the corner of the field outside a wooden hut and watched the others playing.

"I don't know what the hell there is to sing and dance and rejoice about," he shouted to them, "when you should be making yourselves ready for your trial. I am afraid of the damned judge. I think a crazy dragon would be more merciful."

But the officers did not listen to what Major Lawson said; they just kept on dancing and singing.

"You don't seem to be afraid of the damned judge," he went on. "You crazy boys don't know what the judge can do to you. Rejoice and be exceeding glad if you like, but you have not yet felt the damned judge's blow. You had much better pay no attention to what Adam said. I think he is as crazy as you are. That damned judge is more dangerous than you think; he is a hundred times more dangerous than Communism. . . ."

"If you don't dance," said Colonel Asquith, "we shall all tell the judge that you have committed sin incessantly all your life."

"Hell, no you won't," the Major shouted back. "I never committed any sins during my living on earth, so if I can't dance, you certainly shouldn't."

"Make him dance," ordered General Burke. So the officers took him on to the play-ground and made him dance. And he danced and played with the others until a Heaven Plane suddenly appeared and descended on to the field in which they were. And an angel came out from the Heaven Plane and said to them, "Eat your supper right away, then get into this Heaven Plane, for it will take you down to the Judgement Field." And so saying the angel vanished.

The officers hurried into their huts and ate a supper of dried fruits. Then coming out, they mounted the Heaven Plane, which at once flew into the air. And it kept on flying down towards the Judgement Field, flying throughout the night. And the officers slept.

* * * * * * *

News in the Judgement Field

It was just morning and round about half past seven. The Judge was sitting on his chair behind his desk. He was looking intently into the Holy Book which was lying on the desk in front of him. He was still judging Devil-Third, who was sitting opposite him in a condemnation chair. The Holy Agency was sitting on the right of Devil-Third and was defending him diligently.

"You are condemned to be imprisoned in Hell for ever," said the Judge, lifting up his head. "You have committed four Heavy-Mortal Sins, eight hundred and twenty-one Usual-Mortal Sins and ninety thousand eight hundred and twenty-eight Venial-Sins. Your four Heavy-Mortal Sins are these: One, you caused the Harvesting-Living-War. Two, you caused the death of one third of various kinds of earthly creatures. Three, you filled a large number of people with evil. Four, you persecuted many people's souls and their funds."

The Holy Agency stood up and defended Devil-Third diligently. "Never before have you condemned any of the Children of Man in to Hell for ever," he said to the Judge. "I certainly agree that I have seen none more dangerous and sinful, but as he is one of the Children of Man, I hope that you will forgive him some of his sins. Although his sins are numberless, he has done a lot of goodness."

And the Holy Agency said many other things to the Judge in defence of Devil-Third. The Judge looked thoughtfully into the Holy Book for some minutes.

"All your Venial Sins are forgiven for the sake of the Holy Agency," he said at length, "but you are still condemned to be imprisoned in Hell for ever on account of your four Heavy-Mortal Sins and your Usual-Mortal Sins."

"When I said forgive him some of his sins," protested the Holy Agency, "I meant that Devil-Third should not be condemned into Hell for ever. I would be very grateful if you could forgive a few more of them."

The Judge was silent for a long time. At last he spoke. "All your Usual-Mortal Sins are forgiven for the sake of the Holy Agency," he said, "but you are now condemned into Hell for six Heavenly years and two Heavenly months on account of your four Heavy-Mortal Sins."

"I am very sorry that I can't do better than that," said the Holy Agency turning to Devil-Third, "but your four Heavy-Mortal Sins are unforgivable."

"I know quite well that you and this Judge are reactionaries," said Devil-Third angrily. "I was exceedingly glad to leave earth, for I thought that I should not see any of your sort any more. But now I get up here and see you."

He continued to talk thus for some time but neither the Judge nor the Holy Agency answered him one word. Then suddenly a Hell-Plane appeared before the Judge, Devil-Third was hustled in and it flew off without more ado.

"Phew!" said the Holy Agency when it had gone. "I'm tired out after that."

"So am I," said the Judge. "Certainly the greatest trial I have ever judged."

Suddenly the Heaven Plane in which the officers were descended into the Judgement Field. The officers at once dismounted and saluted the Judge and the Holy Agency, who beckoned to them to sit upon the Trial-Chairs. But as soon as they sat down each of them remembered all that he had done during his living on earth.

There was silence. And the Judge looked long and thoughtfully into his Book. Then raising his head he looked solemnly at General Burke.

"Do you confess your four hundred and two Venial Sins and one Mortal Sin?" he asked.

"I confess all my Venial Sins," answered the General, "but I can't confess my Mortal Sin, because I can't remember it."

"Your Mortal Sin is this," said the Judge, consulting the Holy Book. "On the evening of the second of October nineteen twenty-four you were walking along the streets of Washington and you saw a British girl in front of you. You not only looked at her licentiously from time to time but you followed her wherever she went."

"Oh. I see," said General Burke. "I thought that was a Venial Sin. I did not look at her licentiously anyway. I had fallen in love with her; she seemed to me the most beautiful girl I had ever seen."

"Besides falling in love with her, you looked at her licentiously," said the Judge sternly. "And that is a Mortal Sin."

"All right," agreed General Burke. "I confess it as a Mortal Sin. But I did fall in love with her and what is more, you would have done so if you had been in my place. You would have gone crazy. You would give your Judgement Field for her, if she were here now."

"I am exceedingly glad that I was not in your place," said the Judge drily. "Now you are condemned to twenty earthly years' imprisonment in Hell for your four hundred and two Venial Sins and one Mortal Sin."

"Now you," he continued, turning towards Colonel Asquith. "You are committed with two thousand and forty-six Venial Sins and one Mortal Sin. Do you confess them?"

"I don't remember my Mortal one," replied Colonel Asquith, "but I confess all the others."

"When you were at Amirabad Post," explained the Judge, "you promised faithfully that you would give Gunga Din a certificate. But you left Persia without doing so. So it is a Mortal Sin."

"Oh, excuse me. I forgot about that," said Colonel Asquith humbly.

"Twenty-five earthly years in Hell," announced the Judge. "Now you. Two thousand and eight Venial and one Mortal," he went on, looking towards Colonel Wyman. "Do you confess them?"

"Not the Mortal one," answered the Colonel. "What was that?"

"In Amirabad. Gunga Din worked for you for some weeks, but you did not give him anything."

"When the hell did Gunga Din work for me?" asked the Colonel indignantly. "I had another Houseboy. Gunga Din wasn't my Houseboy."

"He was not your Houseboy, but he worked for

you every time your Houseboy took a day off."

"Oh," said Colonel Wyman. "I see. I'm sorry about that."

"Twenty earthly years in Hell," said the Judge and then turned his attention to Colonel Grant. "Forty nine thousand eight hundred and twenty-three Venial Sins," he said.

"Hell. Yes. I suppose so," Colonel Grant agreed.

"Eight earthly years in Hell," said the Judge. "You next," he continued after a short pause to glance at his Book. It was Major Hemming's turn. "Forty-three Venial. Confess?"

"I confess," said Major Hemming.

"Two earthly hours and thirty earthly minutes in Hell," ordered the Judge. Major Matthews followed him. He had one hundred thousand and sixty-two Venial Sins and one Mortal Sin.

"I confess all but the Mortal Sin," said Major Matthews. "What was that?"

"Shortly before you left Persia, you kept yourself in secret and diligently out of the sight of Gunga Din, lest he should ask you to give him any gift."

"Oh. I see. I'm sorry about that," said Major Matthews.

"Six earthly years in Hell," said the Judge.

Captain Rudd came next. Half a million Venial Sins and one Mortal. Like his predecessors he confessed all but the Mortal Sin and asked what that was.

"You have drunk whisky and wine almost without ceasing," explained the Judge.

"Everybody drinks whisky and wine," said Captain Rudd.

"Most people drink moderately," said the Judge. "During your life on earth, you have consumed the following amounts." He consulted his book and then continued. "Whisky 62 tons, Wines 40 tons, various kinds of grogs 53 tons—"

"Yes," said Captain Rudd before he could finish, "I suppose it is a Mortal Sin. I'm sorry."

"Twenty-two earthly years and two earthly months in Hell."

Major Lawson was next. "Three million Venial Sins and two Mortal Sins," said the Judge. "Do you confess them?"

"And where the hell have I got all these sins from anyway? I—"

"Do you confess them?" repeated the Judge.

"I confess my Venial Sins, because I am obliged to," said Major Lawson reluctantly, "but I certainly don't confess the two Mortal Ones."

The Judge ran his finger down a page of his Book. "One evening when you were living at Amirabad Post," he said, "you took the Lord's name in vain while you were taking a shower. You—"

"I— I— Let me— Wait. I want to tell you some-thing," interrupted Major Lawson.

"Say on," said the Judge.

"It wasn't my fault that I took the Lord's name in vain during my shower. It was Major Curtis's fault, for he suddenly turned the cold water off after he had turned all the damned hot water on. I was so angry when the hot water was poured down upon me that I took the Lord's name in vain."

"You should not take the Lord's name in vain even if you are angry," said the Judge. "It is still a Mortal Sin. Your second Mortal Sin is just the same. One holiday you made a trip out of Chicago and the rain began to fall. You gave up your trip and began to run back to Chicago, repeatedly taking the Lord's name in vain as you ran."

"Yes, I suppose I confess it," said Major Lawson, "but it was not my fault really, because the rain was heavy and I had no overcoat with me and—"

"Twenty-eight earthly years and seven earthly months in Hell," ordered the Judge and turned with-out more ado to Captain Birch. "You don't seem to have any sins at all to speak of," he said. "All your deeds seem to have been excellent, so you'll go up to Heaven pretty soon."

He turned over a few pages and then looked to-wards Gunga Din. "Now you," he said and paused thoughtfully. "You," he said, "are condemned into Hell for 96 earthly years. That is for ten million Venial Sins and six Mortal Sins. I expect you know what they all are. Your Mortal Sins, for example. Let me see." He consulted his Book again. "Yes, here we are. When you were working for these officers as Houseboy at Amirabad Post, you used to drink the officers' beer secretly every day. And when the officers asked you what had happened to their beer, you answered that the bottles must have burst through the coldness of the ice. You also accepted many gifts from the officers without working very hard for them. Also your greatest desire was that the Harvesting-Living-War would start soon and that you would see it start with your own eyes."

And so the trial went on until all the officers had been tried. And they were all condemned into Hell save Captain Birch. And when the Judge had finished speaking the Holy Agency arose and began to defend the officers.

"These boys have sincerely been serving Humanity during their living on earth," he said, "and they are very worthiable, because of their good and excellent deeds. And their faith too was pretty good." And the Holy Agency said many other such things to the Judge as he sought to defend them. And after a while the Judge looked into his Book and sat for some time in deep and silent thought. At length he lifted up his head. "You are all forgiven your Mortal Sins for the sake of the Holy Agency," he announced, "but will be condemned into Hell according to your Venial Sins."

At once all the officers began to defend themselves.

"Please look again into that damned book on that damned desk of yours," said Major Lawson. Then quickly turning to the Holy Agency he added, "And you talk to the damned judge some more. Explain to him our supreme services to Democracy during our damned living on the damned earth." He turned quickly back to the Judge. "I would forgive everybody his sins, if I was in your damned place. But I don't see much generousness from you. I think I'm more damned generous than you are."

"You only talk about our sins," pointed out Colonel Wyman, "and you have hidden our good and supreme deeds. We regretfully don't know what is the matter with you that you don't mention our good deeds."

"Yes," agreed Captain Rudd, "you have forgotten all my good deeds but you haven't yet forgotten about my drinking whisky."

"Now let me tell you something," said Colonel Grant. "I don't trust you and I don't believe what is written in that book. And we don't want you to judge us; we want to be judged by the Holy Agency."

"I shall not let Captain Birch go up to Heaven," declared Captain Blore. "Neither shall I let you give him his Freedom Pass."

"You can't stop me," said Captain Birch.

"I certainly can," said Captain Blore angrily.

"O, you're crazy," said Captain Birch.

"Who's crazy?" said Captain Blore, and rising up he threw his Condemnation Chair at Captain Birch. Captain Birch quickly held down his head and the chair, passing over him, struck Colonel Asquith on the breast.

"You foolish boy!" said Colonel Asquith, picking up the chair. "You want to fight with everybody." And he threw the chair back at Captain Blore. But Captain Blore dodged it and it struck Colonel Grant. "Damn you, Colonel Asquith. Are you going mad?" shouted Colonel Grant and threw the chair back at him. This time Colonel Asquith dodged and the Condemnation Chair struck Major Lawson's ear. "O, this damned Condemnation Chair has caused my death! O! O! Alas!" said Major Lawson with pain and he fell down in a faint.

"No fighting in here," said the Judge and then turning to Major Lawson he added severely, "Get up. Nothing has happened to you. You haven't fainted. You are just pretending."

But Major Lawson did not speak. He remained motionless on the floor.

"I won't defend you if you don't get up," said the Holy Agency, "but I will do my best for you if you do."

This time Major Lawson began to move very slowly, saying with great pain to the officers, "O, get me up, please, will you? OO!" Some of the officers at once came to his aid and helped him to sit in his Condemnation Chair. Then he turned his head sadly and painfully to the Judge and asked, "Is there any hospital down there in Hell?"

"There is no hospital in Hell," said the Judge.

"OO! oo! And, and is there any hospital round about this damned Judgement Field?" groaned Major Lawson.

"No. There is no hospital round about this Judgement Field either," said the Judge.

"Well, I can't go down to Hell for the present as I am seriously hurt," went on the Major miserably. "I had better live somewhere round here for some days or weeks until I am better. Will you fix it for me?"

"There is nothing at all the matter with you," said the Judge. "You are just keeping yourself in pain to avoid going to Hell."

NO HEAVEN FOR GUNGA DIN

"Keep quiet," persisted the Holy Agency. "I am going to defend you."

"Oh. Thank you very much. I am keeping quiet," said the Major quickly, and he added, "I hope you win."

And the Holy Agency began to defend all the officers saying to the Judge, "I would be very grateful if you forgive these boys all their sins because their good deeds are very excellent, specially as they were prepared to sacrifice themselves for Freedom." And the Holy Agency stated many other such things to the Judge, so many that I am unable to write them all. And when he had finished the Judge looked into his Book for some minutes. Then he lifted up his head to the officers and he said to them, "As your good deeds are very excellent and as the Holy Agency would like you to go up to Heaven, all your sins are forgiven you. So I will give you Freedom Passes and will send you up to Heaven. But before I do so you shall go to Purgatory by Purgat-plane. And you shall take a shower in the Pond of Purgatory lasting fourteen earthly minutes."

And he said many other such things to them and they rejoiced and were exceeding glad. And then turning to Gunga Din, the Judge said to him, "All your Venial Sins are forgiven you for the sake of the Holy Agency. But your Mortal Sins cannot be forgiven and you are condemned into Hell for forty earthly years."

When they heard these words the officers at once began to defend Gunga Din, saying "Please forgive Gunga Din his Mortal Sins also, for he is a faithful man; he has worked for us for a long time and we have not seen anything wrong with him." And they said many other such things but the Judge interrupted and said, "You cannot defend Gunga Din, for the Children of Man are not allowed to defend themselves, neither are they allowed to defend one another."

And the officers answered, "Excuse us. We will not defend Gunga Din any more but we are exceeding glad to excuse him for all that he stole from us during his working as a Houseboy."

"I won't excuse him," said Major Lawson. "He was stealing my beer, cigarettes and candies all the damned time."

"I am not going to defend Gunga Din," said Major Hemming. "Only I can't help believing that he has a great and wonderful faith in God."

"I am not going to defend Gunga Din either," said Major Matthews, "but there is one thing I must say and that is that I saw him going to church every day with my own eyes."

"And I'm not going to defend him any more," put

in Colonel Asquith, "but to the best of my knowledge his deeds were supreme; he always wished democracy although he could not serve it."

"We will certainly be happier up there in Heaven if Gunga Din is up there with us," said General Burke. "After all, we always have loved our workers much more than they have worked for us."

And Colonel Wyman added, "It is certainly not just that Gunga Din should go to Hell, when he was a poor worker all his days upon earth."

"Keep quiet," said the Judge. "You are defending him and that is strictly forbidden."

"All right. Excuse us, please," said the officers and they kept quiet.

Then turning to the Judge, the Holy Agency resumed his defence of Gunga Din.

"Those Children of Man who are poor and have many labours and troubles during their living down there on earth, should not be condemned into Hell," he said. "Gunga Din was only sinful because of the grievous position he was in, during his earthly living. I confess that his Mortal Sins are grievous and heavy; but I also confess that his good deeds are excellent." And the Holy Agency said many other such things to the Judge. And when he had finished the Judge looked thoughtfully into his Book for some minutes.

"All right," he said at length. "You are forgiven four of your Mortal Sins for the sake of the Holy Agency and because of your good deeds. But your two great Mortal Sins are unforgivable. Now you are condemned to be imprisoned into Hell for ten years."

"I do not think that his two great Mortal Sins are unforgivable," the Holy Agency began again. "I consider them definitely forgivable, because Gunga Din was not a politician, neither was he the leader of any faction or religion during his living upon earth. He was, throughout his life, a poor labourer."

The Judge turned to the Holy Agency. "I am not condemning him into Hell simply because of his two Mortal Sins," he said. "I am condemning him because of his great and wicked desire. And his great and wicked desire was that he wished that the Harvesting-Living-War would happen soon. And that desire is a Mortal Sin, so he must go to Hell."

"Perhaps Gunga Din knew that there could be no peace before the Harvesting-Living-War was fought," suggested the Holy Agency.

"He knew nothing of the sort," said the Judge. "He only wanted to work for the British and American forces again."

"I'm sorry," said the Holy Agency to Gunga Din, "but I cannot defend you any more."

Suddenly a Hell-plane was ready before the Judge

and immediately Gunga Din was taken into it. And all the officers were very sad for Gunga Din, some of them weeping for him. And as the Hell-plane was about to fly away Gunga Din shouted with a loud voice saying, "You have made a great mistake in your judging; I am Gunga Din the Carrier!"

At once the Judge ordered the Hell-plane to be stopped and he hurriedly pushed the pages of his Book this way and that for some minutes. At last he lifted up his head and answered Gunga Din with a loud voice saying, "No, you are not Gunga Din the Carrier. Gunga Din the Carrier was an Indian man. He is now up there in Heaven and he is very happy."

And the Hell-plane flew into the air and continued to fly down to Hell with Gunga Din inside it. And the officers looked sadly after the Hell-plane until it was lost from sight.

"We shall never get another Houseboy like Gunga Din," said some of them.

"Never such a faithful one," said others. And others said, "Gunga Din was an unlikened Houseboy during the whole of life on earth. He was the highest servant. His whole body was knowledge instead of flesh and bone."

"I just don't know what to do for a Houseboy now," said Major Lawson, turning to the Judge. "Can we get any Houseboy up there in Heaven?"

"You will not need a Houseboy up there in Heaven," said the Judge. "Everything you want there will be ready for you."

Suddenly a Purgat-plane was ready before the Judge and the officers arose and entered it. And immediately it flew into the air and continued to fly to the Pond of Purgatory with the officers inside it. And when it reached the Pond of Purgatory the officers dismounted. And they entered the pond, swimming in the water.

"O! The water is too damned hot," said Major Plummer in pain.

"It must be more than twenty times more hot than the usual damned hot water," complained Major Lawson in agony.

"O! I'm going to be burnt up," groaned Colonel Wyman. "What time is it?"

"Two minutes past seven," said General Burke, looking at his watch as he swam.

"O Hell! My skin is burning!" whined Colonel Grant.

"What time is it now?" asked Major Hemming.

"Three minutes past seven," replied Colonel Asquith painfully.

"O! O! I'm going to die. Certainly I am," sobbed Major Lawson. "O, look at your watch again!"

"It's now four minutes past seven," answered

General Burke. "We must swim in this damned water for another ten minutes."

And all the officers were in great pain during their swimming in the Pond of Purgatory.

"If the Wind Commander only knew," groaned Colonel Wyman. "He would make a cold wind blow throughout this damned water-pond. O! O!"

"Look at your damned watch again, General," said Colonel Grant.

"I can't look at my watch from minute to minute during my swimming," said General Burke irritably. "It is now five and a half minutes past seven."

"O, I'm burning, I'm burning," wailed Major Matthews and turning to General Burke he added, "Why the Hell don't you keep on looking at your watch?"

"I shall throw my damned watch away, if you cackle and talk any more," said the General in pain and anger. "It is now six damned minutes past seven."

"That damned judge was our enemy," said Captain Rudd.

"I'm dying, I'm dying," gasped Captain Duff. "How much longer must I last?"

"It is now eight minutes past seven," said General Burke.

"O look! Look!" shouted Major Mandell. "My flesh is boiling just like beef!"

"O Hell!" said General Burke. "Now my watch won't work. It has stopped altogether."

"So has mine," said Colonel Asquith.

"Now nobody has a watch," groaned all the officers and they began to cry in their agony as they swam and swam in the Pond of Purgatory. And their pain increased until they all fainted. And their fainting lasted until the fourteen minutes were ended. And when they were ended there suddenly appeared a beautiful fey. And as she stood over the officers at the edge of the pond she made a sound. And her voice was so infinitely beautiful that all the officers were at once brought round. And the officers so lost themselves as they gazed at the beautiful fey that they might have been swimming in cold water instead of the water of the Pond of Purgatory.

"You can get out now, for your fourteen minutes are finished," said the beautiful fey to the officers. And so saying she disappeared.

The officers came out of the pond and they re-entered the Purgat-plane. And immediately it flew into the air and continued to fly until it reached the Judgement Field. There they dismounted and received their Freedom Passes from the Judge. Ten minutes later a Heaven-plane appeared and the officers entered it. It flew into the air and continued to fly until it reached Heaven. And at last the officers entered Heaven and they were all happy. They visited all the Children of Man who were there and they specially went to Adam's house every day. And all the Children of Man who were in Heaven visited the officers every day. And all the Heaven-creatures —especially the Heaven M.P.s—visited them several times for they wanted to see and look at the Outlaw-Children-of-the-White-Forest. I am not able to write exactly anything about the situation of the officers in Heaven. I only know that they were all happy, all lucky, all pleased and all exceedingly glad during their living up there in Heaven.

One afternoon the officers were sleeping in their Heavenly House. And when they awoke they came into their Resting room. And sitting down they all looked a little sad.

"I have just had a dream about poor Gunga Din," said Major Hemming sadly. "I dreamed I was walking in a large desert. Suddenly I saw a drift of fire and inside the drift of fire I saw poor Gunga Din. And his body was being burnt. And I said unto him, 'Gunga Din, who has cast you into this drift of fire?' But when he wanted to speak and to answer me I awoke."

"I too had a dream," said Colonel Asquith sadly. "I dreamed I was sitting in a chair, reading a book. Suddenly I heard a grievous cry, weeping grievously.

Immediately I looked in the direction of the cry and I saw Gunga Din running this way and that with his body covered with fire. Immediately I rose up to put out the fires that covered Gunga Din's body. But as I did so I awoke and found myself on my bed."

"I, also, dreamed a dream," said Major Matthews. "I dreamed that I was walking in front of a kitchen. Suddenly Gunga Din cried to me in great pain saying to me, "Major Matthews! Please save me." At once I ran into the kitchen and I saw Gunga Din in the oven fire with his hands tied. And I put my hands into the oven fire to pull Gunga Din out, but as I did so I awoke and found that I was upon my bed."

"I dreamed," said General Burke sadly, "that I had decided to go out from my house for a walk. I called to Gunga Din to come and shine my shoes, but however much I called, Gunga Din did not answer me. I began to search for him thinking that perhaps he was sleeping. After I had searched for some minutes I suddenly saw him lying down in the corner of the courtyard like dead. I began to inspect his body to ascertain what had caused his death, but I suddenly awoke and found myself on my bed."

"I had a damned dream too," said Major Lawson. "I dreamed I was taking a bath in the damned bath house. I called Gunga Din in order to tell him that the damned water was cold. But however loudly I

called, Gunga Din did not answer. I came out of the
bath house in order to break Gunga Din's damned
neck, but wherever I looked I could not find him, so
I angrily entered the fire-room of the bath house to
put some wood on the fire. Suddenly I saw Gunga
Din's body on the fire being burnt. I was just about
to pull his body off the fire when I awoke and found
myself on my damned bed in this damned afternoon."

And all the officers had had dreams about Gunga
Din and they told their dreams one after another.
And when they had done so they resolved to go
down to Hell to see Gunga Din. They went to Adam
their Papa and they told him what they wanted to
do. And Adam went to Messenger-Gabriel and man-
aged to get a permission-note for the officers to go.

When the world became night, a Heaven-plane
descended down to the officers' house and when they
had entered it it flew into the air. And it continued
to fly down to Hell throughout the night with the
officers inside it. Just as the world was becoming
morning it descended down to the Gate of Hell. The
officers dismounted. And they came to the Hell-
keeper, who was standing at the Hell-Gate, and they
said to him, "We want to visit a Hellish who was our
servant." And the Hell-keeper answered and said to
the officers, "You must see the Hell-Governor first.

That's his office up there." So all the officers went up to the office of the Hell-Governor. The Hell-Governor was sitting in a chair behind the desk in his office.

"Good morning," said all the officers coming in suddenly.

"Good morning," said the Hell-Governor lifting up his head.

General Burke put the permission-note on the desk before the Hell-Governor, saying to him, "There is a fellow-hellish of ours here and we have come to see him."

The Hell-Governor took the permission-note in his hand. He looked at it, then he gave it back to General Burke. "What is the number of your fellow-hellish?" he asked him.

"We don't know his number," replied the General.

"Then what is his name?"

"His name is Gunga Din," answered the General.

The Hell-Governor opened a large book on his desk and began to push the pages this way and that, searching for Gunga Din's name. Twenty minutes passed. "Ah," said the Hell-Governor at last. "I've got the number of your hellish-fellow." He clapped his hands and at once some Hell-keepers entered. "Bring Hellish Number thirty million and two to

Hell-Gate," he ordered them. "These boys want to see him."

"All right," said the Hell-Keepers and they went out quickly from the office.

"Now go to Hell-Gate," said the Hell-Governor when they had gone, "and wait until your hellish-fellow comes."

"Thank you very much," said all the officers and going out they walked until they came somewhere opposite Hell-Gate. And there they stopped and talked as they looked into Hell through Hell-Gate. And they saw thousands and thousands of black hellishes walking this way and that in the front part of Hell.

"Hell looks like an African city, for all the hellishes are black," said General Burke.

"We shall not know Gunga Din when we see him," said Major Matthews, "for he will certainly be as black as the rest."

"Gunga Din was naturally black from the old days," said Colonel Asquith. And they continued to talk about such things. Suddenly a black hellish came quickly out from Hell-Gate and he came up to the officers saying, "Good morning. I am Gunga Din."

"O, hello Gunga Din. How are you?" said all the officers, shaking Gunga Din's hands. "Sit down here and tell us all about your situation and the situation here in Hell."

And all the officers sat down round about Gunga Din. And they put the Heavenly Eatables, which they had brought for Gunga Din, down before him. And eating the Heavenly Eatables, he began to state to the officers all about the situation of the Hellishes in Hell. "Hell-Fire," he said, "usually attacks us from supper time until morning. By morning it has killed us and turned us into ashes. When the world becomes morning Hell-Fire goes off and we are brought to life again by the power of a voice until suppertime. It is the fire that has made us so black. All the other hellishes are as black as I am. We get rations once every morning and we are allowed to walk about in Hell from the morning until the evening. But we have to be back in the evening. But we have to be back in our own rooms before Hell-Fire attacks. On Holy Days Hell-Fire does not attack us, so then we are a little comforted. We also get rations three times on each Holy Day. There are thirty million and two of us here. Most of them are Communists. Devil-Third and I are the newest hellishes." And Gunga Din stated so many other things to the officers that I am not able to write them all. And his statement lasted 3 hours. And all the officers were exceedingly sad for the Hellishes. They stayed with Gunga Din until the evening and then they left him after they had shaken him by the hand and comforted him. They watched him go back through the Gate of Hell and then they mounted their Heaven-plane. It flew into the air and continued to fly throughout the night. When the world became morning, it descended down to Adam's Heavenly House. The officers dismounted from the Heaven-plane and coming to Adam they told him all about the situation of the hellishes and those of the hellishes who were his own children. And Adam wept with a loud voice for those of his children who were in Hell. And the officers' statements to Adam were so wonderfully noised abroad that all the Children of Man who were in Heaven heard it. So all the Children of Man who were in Heaven were exceedingly sad for those Children of Man who were in Hell. And one day all the Children of Man who were in Heaven gathered together round about Adam's Heavenly house and they took these decisions:

1. That all the Hellishes should come up to Heaven immediately.
2. That Hell must be destroyed.
3. That the Judge must be discharged for ever and the Judgement Field be destroyed for ever.
4. That those Children of Man who were yet on Earth should come directly to Heaven.

5. That Purgatory should be destroyed for ever.
6. That the Children of Man's rank should be more
   excellent than all other creatures.
7. That the Children of Man should be more dear
   than all other creatures.

When they had taken these decisions, they began
to walk together throughout Heaven, proclaiming
with a loud voice, "Be destroyed Hell! Be destroyed
Purgatory! Be destroyed the Judge!" And so they
shouted with loud voices as they marched through
Heaven. And all the Heavenly creatures began to
look at the Children of Man as they marched. And
the angels looked with them. And some of the angels
said with a loud voice, "The Children of Man seem
to have become crazy this morning!" And the Children of Man were very hard angry when they heard
the words that came out of the angels' mouths. And
they attacked the angels and beat them and there
was almost a pell-mell fight between them. But
Adam stood forth and prevented them. He prevented his children from fighting and his children
ceased from their attack. And Messenger-Gabriel
came to Adam and he said unto him, "Hell-Fire has
gone out for ever. Never will it attack the Hellishes
any more. The Hellishes are turned to their natural
colours and they are not black. Now Hell looks like

an earthly prison and all the Hellishes live like prisoners on Earth."

And the next day the Children of Man were gathered together again outside the house of Adam. And they said to Adam, "If our seven decisions be not done, we ourselves will make these secondary decisions: 1. We will go out from Heaven. 2. We will make cities round about outside Heaven. 3. We will leave Heaven for ever. 4. We will eat by labouring as we did down on earth."

"I will talk to Messenger-Gabriel about that," said Adam, "and I will let you know about it next week."

And the Children of Man were a little comforted when they heard the words that came out from Adam's mouth. And they left him and went to their Heavenly houses.

I am sorry that I have not yet got any more news about the decisions of Adam's children, so I have made an end of the story.

God loves all his creatures in one measure.

END END END END END END END
END END END END END END END